C000126557

The Genetic Deviation Series Book 1:

EMERGENCE

By Stephanie Smith

Thank you for the support in buying my first book! Enjoy the adventure!

Smith x

THE GENETIC DEVIATION SERIES BOOK 1: EMERGENCE copyright © 2022 by Stephanie Smith. All rights reserved. No part of this book may be used or reproduced in any manner without written permission except in the case of brief quotations embodied in critical articles or reviews. This book is a work of fiction. Names, characters, places, organisations and incidents either are the product of the author's imagination or are used fictitiously. Any resemblance to actual persons, living or dead, events or locations is entirely coincidental. Book cover design by Sean Smith. Check out the **Emergence: Book 1 in the Genetic Deviation Series** Facebook page for more information, to contact the author or to find out when Book 2 will be released.

To the real Kat, Ben and Jack. May you all grow up enjoying stories and adventures, just as much as I have. X

Acknowledgements

Thank you to my Husband, Mom and Dad for listening to my constant rambling about this story. Also, for their patience and invaluable feedback, it is greatly appreciated, expect much more rambling to come! Thank you to my Dad, for being the first to read the whole story and giving me the drive to see this through to the end.

Contents

Chapter 1 - Beginnings

Jack

Jack was in an expensive car, moving towards a large, white building with a very high, black-metallic fence surrounding it. The man he assumed to be his father was driving the vehicle, and the lady he believed to be his mother was in a beautiful blue dress and sat in the passenger seat. The car slowed as it came to the large metal gates. After a quick chat with his father, the gates were opened by a man in a smart military uniform. The car pulled up to the building entrance, and the three of them stepped out into the cool night air. Jack was aware of how smartly he was dressed; he was wearing a similar suit to his father, who was in a black suit and tie. He saw his reflection in the car window and was alarmed to realise that he was not looking at his reflection, but he saw another boy who looked to be around the same age, who moved when he did, in the glass. His parents were not his parents either.

Jack and his assumed parents made their way into the building, his mother holding his hand tightly as they walked. They were going to see a show, that's what his father had been saying to him all week. A man from his father's work had given them tickets as thank you for something his father had helped him with. Jack's father said he would get some drinks and be back shortly. A very friendly-looking lady walked up to them, saying hello, that her name was Sabrina and that she would be looking after them that evening.

Sabrina took them to their seats, and Jack and his mother waited for the show to begin.

Jack looked around the room and saw the stage. It had a deep red-stained, wooden floor, a hilly landscape painted on the back wall and lots of lights on the ceiling. Their seats were three of many, all set into levels that formed a semi-circle around the stage. In the middle of the semi-circle, it appeared to be standing room only. Jack guessed that the people there didn't manage to get any seats but really wanted to see this show. Jack noticed that he was in the middle tier of the seats, with two more layers of seats above his but higher up. Each level had fewer and fewer seats.

The lights dimmed just as his father got back and sat in the empty seat beside him. He handed Jack a drink and smiled at him. Jack turned his attention to the stage as light, upbeat music began to play. A group of people appeared, rising slowly from a secret entrance in the floor of the middle of the stage. They were all lined up in a row with huge smiles on their faces and began to dance. Something seemed strange about these people, the way they moved seemed off, but they did have huge smiles on their faces, so Jack assumed they must be happy. The music ended, the dancers stopped dancing, they moved forwards to take a bow...

Jack suddenly had a sharp pain sear in the side of his head. He scrunched up his face as he cried out loud. Hearing a dull thudding and a woman screaming, he clasped his hand to the side of his head and everything went black. Jack woke up, sweating, in bed with his head still hurting. Claire came rushing into the room with an alarmed look on her face. He had shouted out loud in his sleep; she looked concerned. Her usually well-kept hair sticking out at odd angles from sleeping.

"Are you alright, Jack?" she asked, "Did you have another bad dream?"

"I'm okay, Mom. My head just hurts," said Jack; he felt overwhelmed with emotion and started to cry. He could feel the fast heart rate thudding in his chest slowly returning to normal. His mother pulled him in close for a hug.

"It's a good job your father is working away this weekend, try not to worry too much. The pain went away quickly last time; maybe it will do the same again," she said with a small smile and a squeeze. "Don't forget what we talked about last time, too; no one must ever know that you get these headaches and bad dreams, especially your father, okay?"

"Okay, Mom, I'm feeling a bit better now," he said, calming down a little. "I can still go to school tomorrow, can't I? It *is* my first day back at school, and I really want to see Kat."

"As long as you feel better, Honey, then I can't see why not," Jack's mum replied. She kissed him on the head, gave him another slight squeeze and tucked him back into his bed. "Goodnight Jack, I love you," she whispered, and she left the room without a sound.

Six-year-old Jack snuggled down and almost fell asleep immediately. He had a fleeting thought that he had been in that dream before; the pain in his head and the dream felt familiar. This was the third time it had happened in a year, but it had gone now. He thought about seeing his cousin at school the following

9

morning; he was excited to see her as they had not spent much time together in their short lives, and he liked Kat a lot. Jack fell asleep as soon as his head touched the pillow.

Kat

In 2195, people who are different from the general population, those who stand out, are deemed dangerous. They are reported and never seen or heard from again. People learn to keep to themselves, and trust is a rare commodity nowadays. This has always been the way, as far back as people can remember, everyone is tested for 'genetic deviations' at the ages of seven and fourteen. If you are flagged as positive, you are taken away for more testing. Nobody had been taken away in the town of Smythwater for twenty years, but the tests are still always carried out. No one taken away for testing had ever been heard from again. Rumours had it that if the genetic deviation was 'useful' to the government, they would employ you to help humanity and the advancement of the human race. You would be given a very well paid job for the rest of your life. If it is not 'useful', no one knows what will happen to you.

It was said many years ago that almost all the cells in the human body will have fully regenerated every seven to ten years. That was supposed to be a myth, that is what the population are told, that is a lie.

Darwin's theory of evolution sparked the imagination of writers and movie makers. The idea that humans could evolve into much more than just a destructive, bi-pedal species was inspiring. This led to bedtime stories of people with unique traits. People who could heal faster, people who could breathe underwater, people who were even fireproof. These people were always killed in those stories, becoming legends and urban myths as the years went by. Kat knew that these stories were real in her heart of hearts, despite everyone telling her otherwise. Kat loved hearing those stories from her mother before bed. She looked forward to them and always asked for her favourites.

Kat is starting a new year at school. She is seven years old this academic year and will have to take the tests the week after her 7th birthday. Jack, who had just moved back to the city with his Mom and Dad, will be in the same class and celebrates his birthday a week after her. Kat had been awake since the sun had risen, casting a reddish hue into her bedroom. She couldn't go back to sleep; she was too excited. Being finally able to play with other kids again after a long, hot summer, her excitement was rising. She dressed quickly and made her way downstairs to meet her parents for breakfast.

Kat's parents were watching the news on the television when she padded into the sitting room. A man was dressed in a dark blue suit speaking to the camera outside a huge, white building.

"The whole family will be utterly devastated that their boy has tested positive for Genetic Deviations at just seven years old. This is the first positive GD in this town for twenty years. Jacob will be taken to this

11

building, where further tests will be done to determine the extent of his Deviation...."

Kat moved towards her mother, who had her hand covering her mouth at the news. She spotted her and quickly turned off the television. Her father, a tall, dark-haired man with glasses, sat at the breakfast table reading the paper. He turned around at the tv turning off and stood up with a massive smile on his face, just for Kat.

"All set? Are you ready for your first day?" he asked. "I have to go to work early today, so your mother will be taking you to school. You are picking your cousin up on the way, so make sure you eat quickly, so you two aren't late." He crouched down to her height, kissed her on the head and started getting ready to leave. He whispered a few things to his wife before he left, but Kat was not interested in anything except her cereal that popped and turned the milk red.

As she sat in the back of her mother's car on the way to Jack's house, Kat looked excitedly out of the window, watching the houses and trees speed by. She had not seen her cousin Jack since the previous winter when the whole family travelled to see their Grandmother for the holidays. Her mother pulled up outside Jack's home; Kat watched her get out of the car and make her way to the front door. She knocked, waited a moment, and her aunt appeared in the doorway. She was still in her pyjamas and talked quite quickly to her sister. They both looked up and down the street as if they were looking for someone and carried on jabbering. Kat could not hear what they were saying, but she could see that her aunt looked tired. She pushed herself as high as she could in her booster seat, straining to catch her first glimpse of Jack.

After what seemed like forever, Kat's mom made her way back down the path alone. She caught Kat's eye as she was walking and smiled. Her aunt saw her from her front door and waved at her. Kat waved back, and the door closed; just as the car door opened and closed, her mother was back in the car.

"Where's Jack?" Kat asked, "Why isn't he coming?"

"I'm sorry, Sweetheart. Jack is not feeling well today." her mom explained. "Aunty Claire is keeping him off school today to keep an eye on him. Hopefully, he will be in school tomorrow."

She smiled again at Kat and turned to start the car. Kat went back to staring out of the window; she was confused and felt deflated. Her mother had been smiling and seemed to look happy, but there was something in her voice that made her seem sad. Kat spent the rest of the day thinking about Jack and why he was not at school. Hoping that the following day would be the day she finally got to see her cousin again.

It was a whole week before Jack made an appearance at school. He had been placed in the seat next to Kat in class, and the teacher had given Kat some classwork to give to Jack whilst he was away. Her aunt would not let her in the house to see him but said she would pass the work on. The sick note the teacher had been given, explained that he had been off sick with the flu. That was the end of it, no follow-ups, and, thankfully, no one else had caught the flu either.

Chapter 2 – Obstacles

Six weeks had passed since the start of term, and it was Kat's seventh birthday on the coming Saturday. Kat was looking forward to it a great deal; her parents were organising a party for her, some of her classmates were invited. She was talking to Jack about it during their Wednesday Physical Fitness lesson.

"Your party is on the same day as your actual birthday, isn't it, Kat?" asked Jack.

"Yes, it is!" Kat said excitedly. A smile spread across her face at the mention of her birthday. "It's going to be so much fun. Daddy has got a Fairy Princess coming; there's going to be a bouncy castle too!"

"My mom is coming to your house early on Saturday morning to help your mom get things ready," said Jack. He turned to his best friend, who was working with the two cousins this lesson and asked, "Ben, are you coming too?"

"I should be able to come; my dad is not working this weekend, so he said he would bring me," Ben replied with a grin. "I can't wait."

They were working in small groups to complete the school obstacle course, and Ben had joined them. He was a tall, thin boy with short blonde hair and glasses. He had piercing blue eyes and was quite shy, but he had quickly become close friends with Jack, which is why they all joined up together during this lesson. The groups all started the course at staggered times so that there should be enough time for each group to make it through each obstacle before the next group caught up.

The trio started pretty well. The first obstacle was stepping stones over a pond of cold water. This was not a challenge for them, and the group breezed onto the next trial.

The second obstacle was a cargo net covered in leaves and fixed to the ground. Again, the three of them made easy work of the task; they got on all fours, crawled quickly underneath, and moved on.

The next obstacle looked a lot tougher; it was a rope climb onto an eight-foot-high platform with a slide on the other side.

"Erm, I can't climb a rope very well," Ben said, stopping in his tracks and looking up at the platform.

"Don't worry," said Kat. "We will help you. Jack can go first to help pull you up onto the platform, and I will climb underneath you to help stop you from falling, okay?"

"Let's hope it works," said Ben, with a nervous glance behind them, looking for the next group who were just about to start the course.

Jack took a firm grip on the thick, bristly rope and began to climb. He pulled himself up confidently. He made it quickly and easily to the platform and lay down on it, holding an arm over the edge for Ben to grab when he was high enough.

Ben gulped and grabbed the rope as high as he could. However, unlike Jack, he turned to Kat with a look of dread and managed a weak smile.

"You can do it, Ben, don't worry," Kat said with a reassuring smile. "I'll grab the rope as soon as you are high enough, and if you slide down, I can slow your fall and help push you up to Jack."

Ben slowly started making his way up the rope. Eight feet may as well be eight miles to an almost seven-year-old who struggles to climb. His arms were burning already. He felt Kat grab the rope underneath him.

"Come on, Ben!" shouted Jack, his arm stretching out to reach him as far as it would go. He was only a few inches away from being able to get Ben. "Just a bit further!"

Ben was trying harder than he had ever tried at anything in his young life. He had his eyes scrunched up tight in the effort, and the small muscles in his thin arms were trembling. Ben was slowly inching his way up the thick, bristly rope. Kat was on the rope below Ben, pulling herself up as hard as she could in a bid to help push him closer to Jack. He had one of his feet on her shoulders as he wasn't strong enough to hold his whole weight on the rope for long.

"Just....a little....further.." Ben panted and gasped. Almost all his energy had been used up now. He could practically touch Jack's hand; they were millimetres apart. He released his right hand to grab a little higher up the rope when...

"HAHAHA! Look who it is!" shouted a loud, mocking voice from below. "It's little Benny! Make sure you don't fall; we are all watching!" The voice belonged to the class bully, Maya, who had taken a particular disliking to Ben. She bullied him as often as she could, Ben thought it was because he was allocated the seat next to her best friend in class, but no one really knew. The two other girls in her group started giggling.

"Ignore her, Ben; you are so close," encouraged Jack from above him. He was still on the platform above them, stretching towards him with every fibre in his body.

Kat gritted her teeth, and in anger at Maya, she pulled herself up the rope as hard as she could in a bid to get Ben within Jack's reach, so they could complete the obstacle. Her massive effort caught Ben off-guard; he lost his grip and fell backwards to the ground. At the same time, Jack had lunged to try and catch Ben's outstretched hand, and Kat slid back to the bottom of the rough rope. Maya and her friends pushed past the fallen trio, making sure to splash them with mud as they passed them, laughing hysterically.

It took a few moments to register what had happened. Kat looked at her hands and had huge blisters and burns form on her palms, partly from how tight she had been holding onto the rope and pulling on it to support both herself and Ben, and partly from holding onto the rope as she slid down it when Ben fell. She left the rope and made her way over to her fallen friends.

Jack, who had lunged off the platform to grab Ben, had done so face first. He was covered in blood and had managed to knock out a tooth. He had also managed to injure his arm, which, luckily, had taken most of the impact of his eight foot fall. Being cautious with his arm, he pulled himself over to Ben to check on him.

Ben had fallen from a shorter height than Jack, but he had landed on his back. The wind was knocked out

18

of him, and a cut on the back of his head was bleeding. His eyes were closed, and his glasses were broken on the floor next to him. Kat knelt at his side and shook him. He opened his eyes with a faint groan.

"I am so sorry, Ben; I didn't mean for you two to get hurt," she looked at the blood-covered Jack with tears burning in her eyes. "I just wanted to get the rope over and done with." She started to cry. Jack got to his feet and put his arm around his cousin.

"Are you hurt?" Jack asked Kat as she stood up. He saw how she was holding her hands and went to take them in his own when she instinctively pulled them away from him. She shook her head and moved back towards Ben, who rolled onto his side and coughed a little. He felt a little wobbly but managed to sit upright. Jack winced in pain with his arm and held it close to his body.

"I'm okay, Kat. Don't get upset; it was an accident," Ben said. He extended his hand towards her; she leaned forward, grabbed both hands, and pulled him to his feet. "Thanks for the help, though; I wouldn't have made it that far up the rope without you." Dusting himself off and giving her a small smile, he picked up the pieces of his broken glasses, and the three of them started walking towards the starting point of the obstacle course. Ignoring Maya and her two friends who breezed through the challenge, the next group was now making their way to their location.

As the trio arrived back at the starting point, one of their teachers spotted the blood on both Jack and

Ben's clothing, and he immediately started running toward them.

"What happened to you three? Where are you hurt? Are you alright?" the slightly panicked adult asked. "Ben? Where are you bleeding?"

"I'm okay, Sir. We were on the rope challenge, and we fell. I cut my head; Jack has hurt his arm and lost a tooth, though… and Kat…"

"…Is fine, Sir", finished Kat. "It's the boys that need help; I will walk them to the Nurse's office." With questioning looks from Jack and Ben, she marched straight past them both and headed up the path, back towards the school. The teacher pulled himself together at this point and was eyeing them all suspiciously; he had been trained to listen out for anything unusual. As he had neither seen nor heard anything that could lead to an investigation being launched, he decided that the kids were just a little shaken from their mishap and would keep a careful eye on them in the future.

As soon as they were out of sight of the teacher, Jack stopped dead in his tracks, causing the others to stop.

"Show me your hands," he said. He was looking straight at Kat. "You burned them on the rope. I saw it in your face when you came off it. Let me look at them." Kat held out her hands, palms down, and slowly turned them over. There were no injuries to be seen.

"I'm fine. You must have looked wrong or hit your head after the fall." She seemed a little shaken, but everything appeared to be as expected other than that. Jack was confused. He could have sworn he had seen blisters on her hands, but she had proven to them that everything was normal, so he let it slide. He had the beginnings of a headache forming, and his arm was hurting; he needed medical attention soon.

"Come on, guys, my cut is hurting now," Ben said. The bleeding had stopped, but he held his hand to his head as if it could help with his pain. He was squinting his eyes a lot; his glasses couldn't be worn due to them snapping in half; the lenses had shattered too. Kat stood beside him, looped her arm through his, and the group made their way to the medical bay without another word. All of them were still thinking about what had happened. Jack, convinced that Kat had been hurt, resolved to keep a closer eye on his cousin from now on. Ben was worried that his parents would be very annoyed that he had broken his glasses and felt a little confused over the fact that Kat may or may not have been hurt.

On the other hand, Kat was worried that Jack might not have been entirely convinced that she hadn't been injured. She had an enormous secret that had to be kept hidden and resolved to be more discreet.

Kat had started showing healing abilities. She had noticed it for a few weeks now, it appeared that they were getting stronger and that she was healing quicker. She first saw it when she was in the kitchen, loading some dishes and cutlery into the dishwasher for her parents. A knife had been put in the cutlery slot with the blade pointing upwards, and she hadn't realised. She sliced open the palm of her right hand. She shrieked in pain and grabbed a towel as it started to bleed. When her Mom came running into the room, it took her 10 minutes to convince Kat to show her the cut. By the time she peeled off the towel, nothing was to be seen. Kat was confused; her mother was annoyed from being called away from a phone call for what appeared to be nothing. Kat could not explain why the injury had vanished. There was blood on the towel, though; how could she ignore that? She wondered whether she had even cut herself, was she seeing things? Many questions were surrounding why her injury had just disappeared, and none that a nearly seven-year-old could answer without more information.

At the medical bay, the nurse tended to their injuries. As with all head injuries, Ben's cut was not as bad as it had first seemed, it had just bled a lot. Jack's Mom had been called, as his arm was possibly sprained or broken and needed hospital treatment, and there was nothing the nurse could do for his missing tooth. Kat waited in the bay with them until her Aunt came to pick them both up. Ben's father was also called to collect him due to his not seeing without his glasses and his head hurting. He did not seem pleased with Ben.

Chapter 3 – Worries

Jack had appeared back at school with a plaster cast on his arm. He had managed to fracture his arm as he fell. Ben's cut needed no further medical attention, and both arrived back at school the following day. The week passed with much gossip and rumours about what happened, mainly fuelled by Maya. Nonetheless, everyone wanted to sign Jack's cast and looked forward to Kat's party as the whole class had been invited.

Kat and Maya had never really become friends, but as their fathers worked together, her parents had asked her to make sure she got an invite to her party. Kat was unhappy about it, but was determined not to let it ruin her special day.

Becoming seven and fourteen years old is a big deal for children in this day and age. A week after you become seven years old, you are called up for a DNA test to look for Genetic Deviations. In the school year when children turn seven, all pupils have to have a compulsory assembly. This assembly explained that about 200 years ago, people started to emerge with Genetic Deviations which gave them enhanced abilities. These abilities ranged from merely seeing and hearing exceptionally well, to more dangerous skills, including controlling the weather or creating nuclear explosions. They were eventually all neutralised, and the world was finally safe. These people were found to all have a marker in their DNA, which is why the tests were created. The reasoning behind them was to ensure the safety and well-being of the population.

Over time, fewer and fewer people were found with these Genetic Deviations. It was discovered that the deviations started to manifest themselves around the age of seven, developing again by the time the person reached fourteen and then sometimes again at twenty-one years of age. Usually, the third stage of the Genetic Deviation only really applied to ones that were considered more dangerous or complex. Nobody had been recorded to have reached the third stage of a Genetic Deviation in over a century however. Therefore, every person is tested twice in their lifetime. Unless people are reported as suspicious and evidence has been submitted to the Board of Genetic Deviation Investigators.

It was only until recently, when a boy called Jacob Harrison tested positive for GDs, the town of Smythwater had been GD free for twenty years. Cases popped up all over the planet, many of them being in the more developed countries. However, these were usually not too dangerous as the 'Deviants' were picked up early on at the seventh year testing. It is pretty much impossible for these tests to miss anyone with the Deviation; the only way this was possible was if your Deviation had not started manifesting at the time the first test had been taken. The fourteen-year-old testing would pick it up however, provided evidence had not manifested before then to warrant another test beforehand.

Kat awoke early on Saturday morning, excited and looking forward to the party. This had taken up every spare thought in her head since her parents announced they would be throwing her one. She ran downstairs to find her parents in the garden hanging balloons.

"Happy Birthday!" her parents shouted at the same time. Their faces were lit up with huge smiles, her mom threw her arms open wide, and she ran towards her for a hug.

The whole garden had been decorated with large banners reading HAPPY 7TH BIRTHDAY KATHRYN! Balloons and streamers hung from the house, on the fence and along both sides of the lawn. At the bottom of the garden stood a giant pink bouncy castle and tables set up near the house for herself and her classmates to sit once they had arrived.

"Wow! This is amazing!" Kat shrieked. "Thank you so much, Daddy!" she ran to her father, hugged him, then ran back inside to start getting ready. Her mother had followed her into the house and caught up with her in her room.

"I have a present for you, Kathryn; I do hope you like it," she handed Kat a flat, pale blue box. It had a bow on top with a tag that read:

"Our Darling Daughter, hope you have a fantastic birthday! Lots of love, Mom and Dad xxx"

She lifted the lid of the box and gasped. There was a beautiful dress inside; it was a deep shade of blue that matched her eye colour exactly. It was made from a silky material; it shimmered like water in the sunlight and it was as light as a feather.

"Thank you, Mom. It is beautiful." Kat said, beaming at her mother. She gave her Mom another hug and accepted her help in getting ready for the party. It wasn't meant to start for another couple of hours, but Jack did say that he was coming over earlier than the others to help out with his Mom, and it would save her having to get changed later on.

An hour later, the doorbell rang. Jack's grinning face could be seen peering through the clouded glass panel in the door, easily identifiable with his missing tooth. Kat's Mom opened it, and he ran inside to find Kat after shouting a greeting to his aunt. Jack's mom followed behind and hugged her sister in the hallway.

"Hi Liz, how are you doing?" asked Claire. "You look tired."

"Good, thanks; organising this lot has worn me out," Kat's Mom replied. "How are you doing?"

As she hugged her sister, Kat's Mom noticed that Claire felt a little thinner than usual and hugged her a bit tighter than she normally would have. Something was wrong; she felt it in her heart that something was affecting her sister. Liz closed her eyes and concentrated hard, placing her hand gently on the back of her sister's neck. She saw a flash of Jack, crying on his bed in his pyjamas. As they pulled away, she noticed that her brown eyes looked very dark and more lines had crept upon her face; her cheekbones were more pronounced too.

"What's wrong with Jack?" Elizabeth muttered quietly.

"You are not allowed to do that!" Claire whispered, frantically looking around. The hallway was still empty, and all they had for company were the coats hanging up by the door. They could hear their children laughing in the garden.

"It's fine, Claire; what's going on?" Liz asked again. "We can go and talk upstairs if it will make you feel better?" She put her hand on her younger sister's arm to reassure her and smiled, hiding the worry that had started to creep into her mind. Whatever was going on with Jack must be important for her sister to look and feel so terrible.

"I will not speak about it, but I can write it down," she whispered. "With the nature of Steve's work, we could be being followed or bugged or anything. I have learned not to trust anything." Liz nodded, and they made their way into the dining room; she got out some paper a pen, and they both sat down in silence whilst Claire wrote down what was troubling her:

Liz, I am so worried. Jack has started having dreams and waking up with headaches. So far, they have been covered up with a combination of my visions and the sheer luck of Steve being at work when they have happened. I fear we will not be able to hide it forever. It looks like Jack may be a Deviant, but I am still unsure what his power will develop into. I will let you know more when you have time to read my mind, and we will not be missed or disturbed.

Claire slid the piece of paper across the table to her sister and watched her as she read it. Her deep blue eyes moved from side to side and the colour drained from her face. This was dangerous; they needed to act to make sure he wasn't detected. His birthday was next week and his test the week after. She nodded, stood up and walked to the kitchen, where she turned on the hob and burned the piece of paper. She hugged her sister again without another word, and they both made their way into the garden to finish setting up for the party.

Chapter 4 – The Party

Kat's party was in full swing. Her whole class had turned up to enjoy the day; Ben arrived with a vast gift wrapped in orange paper, which he knew was her favourite colour. She thanked him with a big hug and popped his gift on the table with the others. Maya had arrived at the same time her two best friends from the obstacle course arrived. She didn't bring a gift, and only her two friends wished her a happy birthday.

Kat was determined not to let it bother her and continued to enjoy her day. The group played games; they even had the Fairy Princess come to the party who helped them with face paints and hairstyles. Glitter officially covered everywhere, and everyone made their way to the bottom of the garden to play on the bouncy castle before cake and party food.

Ben had managed to get some new lenses in his glasses but still had some tape on the frames to help hold them together after his fall. They had been fixed by his grandad, who had some old glasses lying around that happened to be the same prescription that Ben needed, so he had glued them in for him as a quick fix whilst his parents ordered his new pair which would take a week or two to arrive. Ben's parents did not have a great deal of money; they had six children, with Ben being the youngest, so even though his Dad had a good job and worked for the government with Jack's Dad, he still sometimes struggled to make ends meet. They had managed to order a cheap pair that matched his old ones, but they would have to come from abroad, which is why he had to wait longer for them to arrive.

"This party is great, Kat!" Ben shouted from across the bouncy castle as he jumped; he had the biggest smile on his face, grinning from ear to ear. He was bouncing back and forth along the back of the castle with his arms in the air. His blonde hair was going static from the rubber of the castle, sticking out from his head at every angle.

"Thanks!" Kat shouted back. She was also jumping from side to side but opposite Ben, so they always met in the middle. She couldn't remember having such a fun, happy day with everyone she loved around her. Kat was getting thirsty and had made her way off the castle and back to the top of the garden where there were drinks. As she chugged at her drink she turned to see Maya bouncing into Ben with her knee hitting his stomach. He fell to the floor of the bouncy castle.

"HEY! Leave him alone!" shouted Kat. She dropped her drink on the table, spilling it on the floor and ran to the bottom of the garden, awkwardly clambering back onto the castle and making her way to Ben, who was holding his stomach, facing the wall curled into a ball. Jack, who had heard Kat shout, had also bounced his way over to Ben and made his way towards Maya. Everyone had stopped jumping, and Maya was hastily making her way off the castle towards her friends, who were sitting on the grass nearby.

"He didn't do anything to you, you cow!" shouted Jack. "Why did you hurt him for? You should leave this party; you weren't supposed to be invited anyway!"

29

"It's not my fault he is an annoying, useless baby that needs others to stick up for him!" Maya shouted back, looking a little scared that both Kat and Jack were glaring at her and she was alone. Stumbling off the castle, she headed to her cronies. The whole garden was silent; even the music had stopped. "He can't do anything for himself!"

"Y-Yes, I can!" shouted back Ben. He had managed to catch his breath and made his way off the castle towards Maya himself. Everyone else got off the castle, and Jack, Kat, and Ben were now all standing together on the grass, facing Maya, who had now been reunited by her friends. Ben was flushed, his hair was still standing on end in places because of the static in the castle, and he looked furious. He took another step towards Maya and shouted, "LEAVE. ME. ALONE!" He pushed her with both hands, giving her a slight shock from the static he had managed to generate with his bouncing and she fell onto the floor. She landed on her butt and now had a dirty grass stain on the seat of her flowery dress.

"What's going on, everyone?" Kat's dad had appeared, making his way down to the bottom of the garden, curious to see what they were all up to. "Why has the music stopped? It's time for food and cake now anyway, so grab your shoes and come back up to the tables." Seeing how his hair was still sticking up, he rubbed Ben on the head and got a small electric shock. He pulled Maya to her feet and laughed, and they all made their way to get food.

"That was brave Ben, standing up to her like that," said Jack quietly, as they grabbed their shoes from the foot of the bouncy castle. "She landed flat on the ground with a bump." He giggled.

"She's not going to let you get away with humiliating her in front of everyone like that, though," Kat said with a slight frown. She put on her shoes and stood waiting for Ben to do his laces up.

"That's why we have to get her again, so she knows not to mess with us," said Jack with a slight grin as they headed back to the tables. "I know exactly what to do, but I will need both of your help. Kat, distract her but keep Ben away from her and in plain sight of everyone. I need to go to the bathroom."

He went inside the house, so Kat decided to sit next to Ben, saving a seat for Jack and chatted to some of her other guests. Plates of party food had been put on the tables; there was a wide variety of food on the plates for them, including nuts, crisps, sandwiches and even chicken nuggets. Maya was sitting opposite the two of them with an ugly look on her face. She whispered something to one of her friends, who giggled and turned away; Maya continued to stare angrily at Ben, who tucked into his plate of food without a second glance at the girl who liked to make his life a living hell for no real reason.

Kat's parents came out of the house carrying a large pink and white birthday cake with candles, quickly followed by Jack, who ran around the adults with a curious look on his face and took his seat next to the birthday girl. He started shovelling food into his mouth with a smirk on his face, but before Kat could say anything, her parents lit the cake and placed it in front of her.

Everyone joined in with singing Happy Birthday to Kat, except Maya, of course, who continued to give the three of them dirty looks, and Kat scrunched up her eyes and made her birthday wish. She blew out her candles with one breath, and everyone clapped and cheered. She smiled and thanked everybody.

Kat's Mom took the cake away to cut it up into slices for people to eat; Jack offered to help her hand out pieces, so he left the table and followed her into the house. Kat looked and smiled at Ben whilst everyone continued to enjoy their food.

"Hope you had a nice day, Kat; sorry if I've ruined it," he said quietly. "It has been a great party, though." He seemed a bit more relaxed now he had managed to stand up to Maya for the first time.

No one knows how Maya had started to dislike Ben. Even Ben didn't remember correctly; Kat thought it happened over a year ago and had something to do with Maya falling off a swing. Ben was laughing at something else at that exact moment, and Maya assumed he was laughing at her falling. Even though this wasn't the case, and many people tried to tell her otherwise, she vowed to make Ben's life a misery as best as she could ever since. Even more so now he was sitting next to her best friend in class too.

"You haven't ruined it, Ben; it's been brilliant. I am glad you came, and I have had so much fun." Kat smiled at Ben again and turned to her slice of cake that Jack had put on the table.

"Looks amazing, doesn't it?" said Ben as he was also handed his piece of cake. They were all given a dollop of squirty cream on the plate to eat with the cake too, and he immediately started eating his piece. Jack appeared back at the table with the last three pieces to hand out, one being his own and two for Maya and her friend. He sat down next to Kat and continued eating the food that he had started earlier, leaving his cake to the side for the time being.

"Everything alright, Jack?" asked Ben.

"Yep," said Jack with a mouth full of sandwich, he smiled widely, showing the food inside his mouth, "best party ever!"

"AAAAAHHHH!!" Maya screamed after spraying her friend in the face with a mouthful of her cake and whipped cream. She was coughing and spraying cream everywhere, trying to get all remains of her food out of her mouth. "Who did this?!" she shouted, her streaming eyes searching the people at the party and resting on the only person she had a problem with, within the garden. "It was YOU, wasn't it, Ben?" Maya continued to cough and splutter; her friend's face-paint was ruined with bits of cake and cream, her eyes were beginning to fill with tears.

"That's it, Ben, I *know* it was you; you are going to pay. I am telling my mummy!" she shouted, pointing at him.

"I have no idea what you are talking about!" Ben yelled back, trying not to laugh. "I haven't left the table, so I can't have done anything to your cake."

Kat looked at Jack, sitting next to her, barely breathing with his silent laughing. She put two and two together and realised he had done something to Maya's cake and rolled her eyes, hiding a smile as best as she could.

"It....*haha*....it was....*haha*....it was me, Maya!" Jack managed to get out. He could barely sit upright and had tears streaming down his face. "You just ate shaving foam!"

Everyone else at the table had worked out what had just happened to Maya, and joined in with the laughter now, too, including Ben and Kat.

"I don't care if it *was* you now, Jack," snarled Maya quietly. "Ben is still going to be in trouble for it; I will make sure of that." She stood up and stormed into the house. She demanded that Kat's parents phoned her mother to come and pick her up, leaving the remainder of the guests to enjoy the rest of the party and cake in peace.

Jack had gone back home after the party feeling like a hero. He had managed to stick up for his best friend and, what was even better, was that Ben had found the courage to stick up for himself too. He had started to get a bit of a headache, though, from overeating cake and party food no doubt, and decided that he wanted to go to bed early. He told his mom that he wasn't feeling too good, and she helped him get ready for bed.

"Goodnight, Sweetheart," she said as she kissed him on the head. "Sweet dreams." She left the door propped open slightly and the hall light on so that it gave him a bit of light in his very dark room. He closed his eyes and fell asleep.

Jack felt like he had been running through these hot, unfamiliar streets for some time. His larger feet felt heavy and he felt taller than usual too. Arriving at a car park, he spotted a truck that had not been secured correctly at the back. He looked around and pulled himself inside, feeling grateful for a bit of a rest and shade. Looking inside his backpack, he realised that he was wearing a green and red friendship bracelet and pulled out a large bottle of water. Being careful with how much he drank, he instantly felt his body feel more refreshed.

Looking at his surroundings, he saw tools and parts of computers in various states of disrepair. He heard male voices getting closer to the truck, he pulled some tarpaulin across to hide himself better and stayed as still as he could. The truck doors slammed shut with a bang and the engine roared to life. After some time on the road, Jack peeked out of the gap to see where he was and felt alarmed when he saw a huge city.

Concentrating hard, he put his hand on the side of the truck and scrunched up his eyes. The vehicle suddenly jolted and swayed to the side of the street, grinding to a halt at the audible dismay of the men in the front cabin. Jack stood up, jumped out of the side of the truck and ran, heading in the direction that he had come from in the truck. Feeling a sense of triumph that he had managed to make the vehicle stop. He chanced a quick glance back behind him and saw steam hissing out of the front of the truck. One of the men looked up, saw him and pointed at him:

"HEY! That girl just jumped out of the back of our truck!"

"Go and get her then!" shouted the other man, his head under the bonnet, trying to find the cause of the problem. The first man reached into the front of the truck, grabbed a wrench and started towards Jack.

35

Jack, feeling scared, turned and ran. Panic and adrenaline now pumping through him, his running legs moved faster than they would usually go. The only thought in his head was to not get caught....

Jack's head felt like it was being cleaved in two, he had his bedsheet wrapped around his arms and torso like a strait jacket, restraining him. He was boiling, and his pyjamas were soaked with sweat. His mom had her hand over his mouth and, with her other hand holding a finger over her lips, was signalling for him to be quiet in the dimly lit room.

"Dad is home; please don't make a noise, Honey. It's going to be alright," she whispered, looking a little frightened.

Chapter 5 – The GD Assembly

After the excitement of Kat's party, the rest of the weekend rolled by pretty quickly, and Monday morning appeared as if out of nowhere. Kat, Ben, and Jack were all sitting in class. They were all supposed to be drawing or painting trees in Winter, but their topic of conversation was far too interesting to be creating artwork.

Maya had left the school, or so the rumours were currently saying. According to her friends, Maya had felt humiliated after Jack's prank at the party and she couldn't face coming back to school. Maya's mother worked in the government, she was pretty high up from what they could surmise, so it made sense that she could pull her daughter out of school easily because of her "being bullied'.

"I'm glad she's gone," said Ben with a wide smile. "She won't be around to keep annoying us now."

"Yeah, that's true," said Jack. "The best thing I ever did, making her eat that shaving foam. I nearly died laughing." Jack started to giggle again. "Did you see her face when she spat it out? I will remember that forever." He leaned back in his seat with his eyes shut, replaying the memory in his head again and giggling even more.

"Well, I don't like how she threatened Ben before she left on Saturday," said Kat, her brow furrowed in thought. "She isn't the type of person to just let this go, is she?"

"Ah, she's gone now, Kat. Just leave it will you and stop worrying," said Jack. "She can't touch Ben now that she isn't here."

"Yeah, my parents are happy she is gone now too," said Ben. "Even if her mom works with both my dad and Jack's dad. She won't be invited to any more birthday parties if she isn't in our classes at least."

The three of them continued to draw their winter trees, using as many shades of reds and browns as they could find for their artwork. All was well, until their class was disturbed by the Headteacher and a man in a black suit and tie appearing at the door. Their class teacher nodded and gestured for them to come inside, immediately looking worried.

"Good morning, children; I am so sorry to disturb you all from your work," the Headteacher announced. "Ben Phillips, can you collect all of your things and come with me now, please." The Headteacher looked pale and she gave a long, knowing look at their class teacher, who had quickly got to her feet and made her way towards Ben, helping him gather his belongings.

"Don't forget your coat, Sweetheart, and say goodbye to Kat and Jack," she whispered, squeezing his shoulder gently.

"Bye, guys," Ben said, looking from his teacher to his best friends and feeling confused. "See you tomorrow." He picked up his backpack and turned to his teacher, "I'm ready, Miss," he said.

"You aren't ready for this, Sweetheart, but okay," she said quietly, as she walked with him to the Headteacher, her hand on his shoulder. "Take care, Ben." She sniffed and turned away as he walked innocently through the door, not knowing what he was

38

being called for. She wiped her face smoothly in one motion as she turned, so the rest of the children didn't see the tear she had shed for the sweetest boy in her class.

"You have your test this weekend, Kat, don't you?" asked Jack. They had watched Ben leave the room; their teacher had told them to carry on with their drawings and sat at her desk, head in her hands. She told the class she had a headache. The chatter in the room returned to normal levels once more.

"Yeah, my Mom and Dad are taking me to get it done. I can't wait for it to be over," Kat replied, turning back to her picture.

She had been worrying about it ever since her birthday party had ended and tried hard to stop thinking about it. She knew what would happen; she would walk into a room that had a chair identical to that at the dentist. Kat would have to sit there and take a swab inside her mouth and a blood test. The whole sample collecting would take less than ten minutes. She would then have the results a couple of days after the tests had been run through a machine and examined. The results would be given through the mail within the week. With all her heart, she hoped she would be negative. No one in her family had ever tested positive; she would be fine, her parents kept telling her. She wanted to believe them, she tried a couple of times to talk to Jack about what happened the day they fell at the obstacle course, but she couldn't. She wouldn't be fine, she could not imagine herself making it past the weekend.

"Mine is a week on Friday, so at least we will have them both over and done with together," Jack said, trying to reassure his cousin. "I am not having a birthday party this year, but my mom and dad are throwing me a small "negative GD results" party instead," he continued with a smile. "You will come, won't you?"

"My Mom has said we would be there; your Mom asked her at my party. Is Ben going?" Kat answered. Her pencil crayon had broken, and she was rummaging through their supply pot on their table, looking for a sharpener.

"Yep," he replied, "He is coming to my house for a sleepover the night before, so he will be there when you get there. There isn't anyone else coming, just your family, mine and Ben."

Kat finally found the pencil sharpener and walked to the front of the class, where the bin could be located. She glanced at her teacher, Mrs Green, who seemed sad. She was hurriedly typing something on her computer and looked as though she had been crying. Whatever it was that had upset her, it must have been important.

The rest of the day carried on as usual, ordinary as it could have been anyway. Ben did not appear at school for the rest of that day; Kat and Jack assumed that he had to go home and that they would catch up with him tomorrow.

The next day, Maya was back at school with a whole new air of smugness and hostility towards Jack and Kat. It turned out the rumours were wrong, and she hadn't left the school at all. A whole school assembly had been called for the very first thing that morning. They had another talk about Genetic

Deviation tests to sit through and what to do if you saw someone acting suspiciously.

As the whole school filed into the hall, a man in a black suit and tie stood still at the front of the room. His hair was gelled and slicked to the side and he wore dark framed glasses. His hands were clasped behind his back and he had a companion that stood at the back of the room, watching everyone with a piercing stare as they entered. The menacing man giving the speech, constantly paced the width of the front of the assembly hall whilst he spoke to the whole school in his deep, booming voice.

"If someone you know is acting strangely, doing things they shouldn't be doing or even looking or sounding different to how they usually look or sound… PAY ATTENTION! This could be the signs of a Genetic Deviant. You must report them." The man was tall, with shiny black shoes and his eyes were constantly sweeping along the rows of children before him. He seemed to be angry at having to speak to everyone in the room. As if he had been called away from doing something meaningful to give a presentation to a group of kids he didn't want to talk to. "It doesn't matter who these people are; they could be your brother, sister, teacher or friend. You *must* tell a teacher you can trust or call the GD anonymous helpline, which can be found on displays around the school. You can also find the number on the leaflets you will all be given before you leave for the end of the day. Any questions?"

Kat looked at Jack, who seemed as worried as she thought she looked herself. Not one hand was raised to ask this intimidating man a question. She wondered

41

what happened to the Deviants once they were discovered. Everyone she spoke to could not provide her with a better answer, other than "they are not seen again," or "they go off to help the Government." Kat looked beyond Jack and could see Maya whispering and smirking at her friends a few seats along. Kat had a strong feeling that she might have had something to do with Ben being called out of class the day before.

When they made their way back to their classroom, they realised that Ben was not in school again. Jack even asked the teacher where he was, but she did not answer him; she suggested that he may be ill. Jack didn't believe her; he was worried about his best friend. His teacher didn't even call out his name when taking attendance; she must know what was going on with him.

Maya unnecessarily pushed past Jack to get to her seat on the other side of the classroom. He could feel his temper rising.

"Just ignore her," whispered Kat, "It's not worth it." Kat stared at Maya, crossed her arms and seemed to drift away in her thoughts.

Minutes later, Maya passed by Jack's seat *again* on her way to the teacher's desk during the lesson. Jack watched her and waited. He would get her back for being so awful. He waited patiently, and on her way back to her seat, he quickly stood up, shoving his seat as far behind him as he could. He pinned Maya to the wall, hard, she started crying loudly.

"Jack!" shouted the teacher, standing up and pointing towards the door. "Go to the Headmistress' office, now!" She had seen what Jack had done, but not the antagonistic behaviour leading up to the

42

incident. She leaned on her desk, writing quickly and scribbled a note on a piece of paper; the head mistress' name was written on the front of the message. She stapled it shut and held it out for him. "Take this with you and give it to the Head when you arrive, please."

"Ah, Jack, you've done it now," Kat said, shaking her head, "I'll meet you after school by the gates if you don't come back to class." Jack nodded at his cousin, not meeting her eyes.

"Yes, Miss," Jack said in a low voice, answering his teacher. He stood up, walked the length of the classroom with everyone staring at him and took the note from his teacher. He left the classroom and caught a glimpse of Maya laughing and pointing at him as he closed the door behind him. He felt his anger flare again so he slammed the door shut as hard as he could behind him.

Chapter 6 – Fly On The Wall

Jack took his time walking to the Headmistress' office. He was too angry and far too upset to be worried about being caught in the corridors during lessons. Looking around, stopping in an empty hall, he carefully unbent the staple holding the paper closed and slid the note open. The note said:

Jack Roberts has been sent to you as he has intentionally hurt another student during the lesson. Please keep him with you until the end of the class, then send him back for lunchtime so that I can have a chat with him then. Many thanks, Mrs Green.

Jack carefully fixed the paper closed again, bending the staple back to its' original position and continued on his way. The corridors were empty, and all that could be heard was the murmur of children working on their classroom tasks. The Headmistress had an office on the other side of the school. He had to go outside and walk across the playground to the second part of the school, where the older kids had their classrooms to find it.

Jack was struggling to keep calm. He was feeling a mixture of feelings all at once. He was scared for Ben, worried with all his heart for his best friend. He was angry at Maya. He had never disliked anyone this intensely before; he really wanted to hurt her. He was confused about his headaches too. His nightmares seemed so real. He decided that he would not go to the Head's office but sit in the opposite staff room until the lunch bell rang. Then he would head back to Mrs

Green and Kat, who would probably be waiting for him. Mrs Green would not know that he did not go to the Head.

He opened the staffroom door and looked around. He had only been in here once before, and that was to help another teacher grab some items for another class about a month ago. It was a large room with a microwave and kettle in a small kitchen in the far corner and had lots of old, squashy armchairs dotted around the room in small groups around low tables stained with coffee rings.

He chose a dark blue armchair with gold leaves embroidered onto it. It was well worn with high arms and was in another corner of the room, against the wall, looking towards the kitchen. He put his note on the coffee table next to his chair and settled into his seat, trying to calm his thoughts. He was starting to get a headache, which did not make him feel any better, so he curled up in the chair with his head on the arm, hoping to sleep the pain away.

He could hear talking in the corridor outside; he could see through the glass panels in the door that a tall, blonde teacher was standing with one hand on the door handle and her back to the door, chatting to another teacher. Immediately, Jack dived off his seat and squashed himself quickly between the wall and the side of the chair that he was in.

The pain in his head peaked with an almighty throb, and Jack woke up. The dream seemed so real. His head was still throbbing and, not knowing why he did it, followed his instinct. He squeezed himself between the wall and the chair and hid. No sooner had he done this, he could hear chatting outside and heard

45

the staff room door open. One of the teachers walked into the staffroom and put the kettle on. It was the tall blonde teacher from Jack's dream! Jack's stomach somersaulted, and he stayed put, trying to make himself as small as possible, not making a sound.

The teacher walked around the room, picking up a few cups and straightening cushions whilst she waited for the kettle. She was moving closer and closer to where Jack was hidden; his heart began to race. She had picked a piece of paper from the coffee table near his chair and was about to scrunch it up and put it in the bin, when she realised it had the Headmistress' name on the front. *Mrs Jackson.* It was his note!

Doing exactly what Jack had done with the staple, she bent it out of place and slid open the letter, reading the note his class teacher had written. She glanced around the room quickly and closed the letter, bending the small piece of metal back to its original position. The staffroom door opened again, and another teacher greeted the first teacher warmly. She was older, with curly brown hair and warm brown eyes. They both sat and chatted whilst marking books. It seemed that they were on a free period together.

Jack's legs were starting to ache, sitting in such an uncomfortable, cramped position for what seemed like forever. His headache had begun to fade away now, and so many questions were running through his mind. He was in his own world, far away from the staffroom, when he heard the name of his best friend being said aloud.

"Such a shame what happened to Ben Phillips though; he was a lovely sweet lad," said the brown-haired teacher. "Stacey was devastated when the

46

Headteacher walked in on her lesson on Monday to collect him. Who would have thought it, eh?"

"Yes, I did hear a rumour that the Suits had come for him," replied the blonde teacher. "I didn't think Ben had it in him to be a Deviant. I taught him last year, and he was such a polite, decent young man. Pretty mild-mannered, wanted to do well and eager to please."

"From what I hear, it was Maya Anderson's mother who reported him," said the brown-haired teacher. "She must have had proof he had a deviation; they don't just take anyone who has a finger pointed at them. Although, she is pretty high ranked from what I gather, she may not have needed any proof." The teacher sighed, "Poor Ben." The two women sat silently, and Jack heard one of them sniff a couple of times. He was horrified at what he heard, a knot had started to form in his stomach, and his mouth had dried out completely.

A few minutes later, a bell sounded to mark the end of the lesson and the beginning of lunch. Both teachers packed away their things and left hurriedly, chatting about lunchtime duty. Jack had a few precious seconds to make his way back to Mrs Green and leave the room before anyone else came in. Doing the best an almost seven-year-old could, he held his temper; he moved quickly; he needed to speak to his cousin.

Chapter 7 – Investigations

Jack made his way back to his classroom feeling like he was in a movie, that what he was seeing and hearing wasn't real and everything felt a bit of a blur. His teacher was still in the room, chatting to Kat. They stopped talking as soon as he burst into the room, both of them stared at him. His usually pale, freckled face was flushed red, and his heart was racing.

"I need to speak to you, now," he said to Kat. "In private." He was slowly coming back to his senses and was aware that they were not alone.

"What's the matter?" Kat asked. "What's going on...."

"Excuse me, Jack, but you need to speak to *me* first," Mrs Green interrupted, standing up and moving in front of her desk. "In private," she added, looking at Kat with a small smile. "I would like you to sit and explain to me what is going on with you today."

Kat picked up her backpack and stood outside, waiting for Jack. She had plenty of things worrying her, and her mind was constantly jumping from one worry to the other. It was of the utmost importance that she pass her GD test this Saturday, and Kat could not find any way of getting out of it. She needed help, but had no adult she could trust enough to ask for that help. This is what their Government aimed for, to create a whole community of people who were trained to report anything suspicious. You were putting yourself at risk of being reported for the slightest request that was out of the ordinary and, in Kat's case, this was not a small, unimportant request. She *was* a Deviant and the penalty for anyone known to be helping or hiding a Deviant was severe.

She was also worried about Ben and his disappearance; Jack was not helping her either. Something was bothering Jack, but if he didn't want to explain what it was, she wasn't going to force him to tell her.

The classroom door finally opened, and Jack came out. He had a troubled look on his face and walked quickly ahead of Kat. The corridors were all empty as lunchtime was in full swing, making it easier to get out of the earshot of their teacher faster.

"Jack, where are we going?" asked Kat as she tried to keep up with him. He glanced over his shoulder and motioned for her to follow him; they left the building and headed outside. Kat felt confused at her cousin's behaviour.

The two of them walked quickly around the edge of the playground, ignoring the shouts from fellow classmates to join them in their games. Jack had still not spoken and was slightly ahead of his cousin. He did not want to be spotted by their lunchtime supervisors, so he quickened his pace. There were some fields along the far side of the school that were out of bounds during lunchtime, but if they were quick, they could get there and hide in the bushes along the edges of the field. There they could talk in private where there was little chance that they would have to worry about being overheard.

Finally, Jack came to a stop at the edge of the trees and looked around. He pointed to a large bush just through the trees. They trampled through the nettles and weeds, making their way across the dark red soil, climbing into the thick brush and sat at the bottom of it.

"What's going on, Jack?" Kat asked again. "We shouldn't be out here; we will get caught and we will be in so much deep trouble."

"It's Ben," exclaimed Jack, his chest starting to heave with emotion. "I didn't go to see the Headmistress earlier; I sat in the staffroom. I heard some teachers talking, and they said some people called "Suits" have him. It's all Maya's fault!" He was breathing rather quickly and and punched the ground angrily with his clenched fist. He was furiously blinking away the tears that were stinging the corners of his eyes. Kat moved closer to him and gently put her hand on his arm.

"*She* reported Ben? How? Why?" Kat was confused. "It must have been because of the party...." She looked at Jack; her blue eyes met his brown eyes for a second before he looked to the ground and started sobbing. His best friend had been taken away; he didn't know why. He also didn't understand why Maya hated Ben so much that she would go to such lengths to get him into the serious trouble he was in, it seemed a little too extreme.

The two of them chatted more about what Jack had overheard once he had calmed down a little more. somewhat. They ate their lunch and sat in the red dirt in silence for a while before heading back to class. Jack's talk with Mrs Green was just a check-in to see if Jack was likely to lose his temper again enough to stay in the same room as Maya for the afternoon

50

lessons. The answer had been yes. However, Jack would have to use every bit of self-restraint he had. He had left to hold it together and not get into any more trouble. They dusted the deep red dust off their clothes and hastily headed back towards the school. They needed to come up with a plan to find Ben and do so quickly.

That afternoon, they were all tasked with reading quietly whilst the teacher called them up to her desk for an end of term review. Kat wasn't reading at all, her mind was spinning with what Jack had heard, and she was trying to think of a way that they could find Ben and to see if he was okay. Chewing on her lip, she looked up and glanced across to Maya, who unfortunately looked up at that exact moment too. Kat felt a wave of burning anger rise inside her chest as their eyes locked. She refused to look away, and so did Maya.

"Maya, can you come up to the desk, please?" Mrs Green's voice rang through the air, and Maya flinched. Kat continued to stare at Maya, who glanced back, looking worried. Kat glanced worriedly at Jack, sitting across from her with his back to the wall. He was staring off into space, facing the table. His face was still blotchy from crying earlier, and his whole body language showed how deeply upset he was.

Then the idea hit her. Why doesn't Jack ask his dad what happened to Ben? He is friends with Ben's dad, and they work together. That was it! That problem was solved; Jack's dad would help. He wouldn't let anything happen to Ben; this was all just a mistake. She could now go back to worrying about her Genetic Deviation test.

The school day took forever to end in Jack and Kat's eyes; they grabbed their belongings and headed towards the exit as quickly as possible. Maya barged past the two of them. Not saying a word to either of them and ran the length of the corridor, out the front doors, down the steps and into her mother's giant black car with dark, tinted windows. She drove off almost immediately.

Jack and Kat jumped into the back of Kat's mom's car and fastened themselves in.

"Good day at school, you two?" she asked. Neither of them replied. "That bad, huh?" she chuckled and started the car. There was a traffic diversion on the way home, so she chose a different route to her normal one. Kat sat up straight and pressed her face to the window.

"This is Ben's street!" she said excitedly. "Mom, can we stop off at Ben's to say hello, please? He wasn't in school today."

The car was moving so slowly down the long road; the traffic diversion had diverted a very busy main road. It took a long time for the vehicle to get within sight of Ben's home.

"I can see his house!" said Jack excitedly. His face had broken into a small smile, and his face was pressed into Kat's window, leaning over her to get a glance at his best friend's home. The window was steaming up with his effort. The traffic started crawling along the road once more and ground to a halt immediately outside the house they were looking for. Kat's mom gasped in shock at the large sign that had been hammered into the front lawn.

"The house is up for sale?!" she said, feeling confused. "Since when?"

"WHAT?!" said Jack and Kat at the same time.

"It can't be true; he would have said something if he was moving home," said Jack. His heart was hammering in his chest, and an uncomfortable, heavy blanket of anxiety was slowly wrapping itself tighter and tighter around his whole body, making it hard for him to think clearly or breathe. His hearing had gone funny, he could hear a loud thumping, and everyone sounded like they were underwater. Where was his best friend? What had happened to him?

He didn't remember getting out of the car or saying goodbye to his cousin and aunt. He didn't remember even greeting his mother; he walked straight past her once she had opened the front door and went straight upstairs. He only stopped to remove his shoes to crawl into his bed, where he fell asleep immediately fell asleep, , completely exhausted from the stresses of the day.

Chapter 8 – Jack's dream

Jack had his hands tied together. He was wearing what looked like dark blue pyjamas and had a thick, coarse rope tied tightly to his wrists. The corridor they were walking down was very bright and bare. It reminded him of a hospital. The other end of his rope was held by a tall, brown-haired woman dressed like a doctor in a white coat. Her hair was in a tight ponytail, and she wore glasses that had thick black frames. He had a man walking behind him, dressed in a white coat. He had a badge pinned on his jacket with his photo on it.

They turned a corner and stopped outside a room with a window, looking into the corridor. Jack could see a dentist's chair in the room and had what looked like wide, leather belts attached to it. It had the same lights the dentist used and even had the tiny sink and table next to it. The woman in front of him opened the electronic door electronically with her name tag, pulling him inside with the rope.

There was a mirror on the wall where the window to the corridor should have been and, instead of his reflection, he saw his best friend standing where he was. His heart gave a terrified jolt in his chest. Ben looked so tiny and afraid. His glasses were cracked, his lip was swollen, and he had a black eye. His usual well-kept blonde hair was messy, and he looked as white as a sheet.

"Take a seat," she said in a cold indifferent tone. It wasn't a request, her tone was impersonal and cold. Jack stayed where he was. He had a terrible feeling that this was not a routine dental check-up. "Now," the woman said, with a commanding tone. He was afraid, this lady seemed dangerous to Jack, and he tentatively moved towards the chair. The man behind them made an impatient noise at the lack of compliance and scooped Jack up. He carried him across the rest of the room and slammed in one motion, slamming him into the chair, deftly freeing his wrists. He grabbed the belts that Jack had seen earlier and fastened his arms tightly to the seat. His head, legs and torso were also secured in this fashion. He now couldn't move at all.

"What are you doing?" Jack asked. "Let me go. Please! I haven't done anything wrong. Someone help me!" He tried to push against his restraints and pull against the restraints, but he knew it was futile. A second later, he had a piece of cloth shoved unceremoniously into his mouth by the woman to reduce his talking. The man was rummaging through a drawer, looking for something. The woman had then taken a seat next to the chair Ben was fastened to and connected him to some wires on a machine. It started beeping in time with the beating rushing through Jack's ears. She started typing on a small laptop that was next to her.

"Found it! Finally!" the man said, triumphantly, holding up a small, clear glass bottle.

"Pass it to me, quickly; we need to get this test started," the woman said. "This is going to hurt you a lot more than it will hurt me, little one." She smiled as *she said this, took out a long, thin needle and filled it slowly with the clear liquid.*

Jack was sweating, he couldn't shout for help, and however he had gotten into this situation, it looked like he needed a miracle to get out of it again. He tried again to resist his restraints, but it was no use. He was stuck here. His heart was beating faster than it had ever beaten before, and he knew he was in trouble. These people were here to harm him, and he was all alone.

The woman rolled up his right sleeve and tied a a strip of rubber strip around the top of his arm. She then injected the clear fluid into it. Jack immediately felt like his whole arm was on fire. Intense pain shot from his arm to the rest of his body, he felt his eyes roll into the back of his head. His body stiffened, and absolute pain continued to increase, ravaging through his tiny body, it peaked and he passed out.

"BEN!!" Jack screamed. He woke up, drenched in sweat and tears on his face.

"Ssshhh, calm down, JackSweetheart, calm down." Once more, Jack's mother had been in the room when he woke up. She sat next to him on his bed and stroked his damp hair. "It's going to be alright."

"Mom, it's Ben; I had a nightmare. It was real; I know it was," Jack started. "He needs help; someone has got him and is hurting him."

"I know, Honey. I know. We need to talk. Your father is due back any minute, and I need to tell you something. You must promise me you will never speak about this to anyone, except maybe your cousin. Do you understand?" She looked straight into his eyes, and he nodded.

"Okay, Mom, but we need to help Ben. Now." Jack was adamant that his best friend would not be forgotten. Jack had to help him, no matter what the cost.

"We can't do anything for Ben at this moment, Sweetie, but you need to be very careful yourself. You are a Deviant. That means that you have a power that runs through your genes which could change over time, providing you don't get caught. This must be kept hidden at all costs. You appear to have visions. From what you have described, the nature of these seem to be in real-time, however they may not always be this way. I don't doubt that Ben is in trouble, but *you* are also in very real danger now." She talked very quickly and so quietly that Jack strained to hear her. She kept nervously glancing towards the door, waiting for her husband to walk in.

"So, what is going to happen to me now?" asked Jack nervously. "Will I go where Ben has gone?" His heart had continued to hammer at his rib cage, having not quite recovered from his dream and now from hearing what his mother had to say.

"You know you have a GD test the week after your birthday. You will test negative, don't worry, just trust me on this. There's one more thing, Kat also has the same gene and is a Deviant too. You must both go through the tests, do not let anyone else know what you truly are. We will all get through this; try not to worry."

There was a bang from the closing front door and a jangle where Jack's dad put his keys on the table next to it. "Goodnight, Sweetheart, try not to worry. I love you so much." She kissed him on the head, turned off his light and exited the room as quickly and quietly as she had entered.

Jack could hear his mom and dad talking downstairs, they were louder than usual, and his mom appeared to come upstairs to bed a lot earlier than his dad. He lay awake, his mind whirring, thinking about everything he had just been told. Ben needed his help, but he couldn't get to him. He was being hurt on purpose... Did Ben have deviance too? Kat did have a deviance, though; he had known something wasn't quite right with his cousin; he would speak to her in the morning. He finally fell asleep, hoping to have another dream about his best friend, so he knew whether or not he was alright.

Chapter 9 – Deviants Together

Jack did not bring up the conversation that he had with his mother during the car journey with Kat and his aunt, on the way to school the next day. He decided he would speak to Kat about what he had discovered, when they had time alone. His mother did not want him to go to school today, but he insisted on going to speak to his cousin.

Finally, during their lunch hour, Jack insisted on sneaking into the trees on the edge of the school field again to speak to Kat.

"Please, I need to talk to you; it's very important," he said when Kat questioned why he wanted to go back out of bounds again. He was starting to feel the ever increasingly familiar beginnings of a headache that could lead to him having another bad dream later on. He rubbed his temples and marched off, hoping Kat would follow.

"Okay, I'm coming!" she shouted after him. She grabbed her backpack and set off to catch Jack up. He was almost running across the playground, ignoring calls from classmates who wanted them to join them in their games once again. They did not realise that they were being watched this time; they were followed at a distance. They finally reached their spot by the large bush and sat in the red dirt.

"What's going on, Jack?" asked Kat. She was a little out of breath and worried at how pale her cousin had turned. "Is everything alright?"

"No, I need to tell you something," he said, rubbing his head again, his headache was not getting any better. "We are Deviants. We have powers; my mom told me last night. I had a dream about Ben; it wasn't a dream though. It was real; some doctors were hurting him; that's my power. I see things happen in my dreams that are real. You have power too, but I don't know what yours is."

"I know I have a power," Kat said quietly, looking at the ground. "They are going to take me away after my test...I just know it."

"What power do you...." Jack didn't get to finish his sentence as Kat covered his mouth quickly and put her finger to her lips.

"Sshhh!" she whispered. "I can hear something." Kat had heard voices not too far away, and she started to panic. "We need to hide. Get inside the bush. Now." They grabbed their backpacks and stuffed them into the bush, quickly following them. The two of them lay as still as the air just before a storm breaks. The brush was very thick, so they were well hidden amongst the foliage and shadows that the other trees cast.

"They are here somewhere, I know it!" said a shrill voice. It was Maya, but she was not alone. She had brought along a teacher that taught one of the older year groups. He had been on playground duty that lunchtime. Kat and Jack knew they were out of bounds, but the trouble they would get into for being caught would be nothing compared to the danger they would have been in if they had been overheard. They both needed to be a lot more careful. Staring at each other in the semi-darkness, both of them, at that point, realised how close they were to trouble.

"There is nobody here, Maya." Said the teacher that had accompanied her, looking around the area. He looked slightly annoyed. It was instilled in every person that reporting someone acting suspicious or out of the ordinary was a good thing. That catching and exposing deviants would keep the world in which everyone lived safer. The rewards were far superior to a teaching salary, and any hint of something even slightly suspicious was worth a shot. Many people applied to become teachers in this day and age. You were in the company of lots of young people who could potentially be deviants. They would be very unlikely to control any deviations that may appear at their age, making them easier to spot and cash in on. However, the proof needed to launch an investigation would be harder to get. A couple of kids wandering off during their lunch break would not necessarily mean they were deviants, but it would mean that he needed to keep an eye out in case they were and if he wanted the reward.

"They *are* here; I know they are!" Maya was annoyed; she was frantically scanning the area in the semi-darkness. She wanted to know what Kat and Jack were up to. Walking past the bush the cousins were hiding in, squinting in the poor light, she seemed to be frustrated. After reporting Ben for the birthday party prank, she vowed to make them pay for humiliating her too.

"Maybe they went somewhere else?" suggested the teacher. "Maybe you were mistaken in guessing where they were going?" He gave the area one last sweep and slowly started making his way back to his duty spot in the playground.

"But Sir, please..." Maya sounded desperate. "We can find them..." She walked towards the teacher, almost pleading with him.

"You need to come along now, Maya. You will be out of bounds if you stay here alone," he said sternly. "Let the matter drop now. I am sure your classmates will be either eating lunch or in the playground when we get back." They made their way back to the school, and Maya's whining and pleading could be heard, getting fainter as they walked away.

Jack and Kat were frozen in fear in their hiding spot. The reality of their situation had started to take effect, and they were still staring at each other.

"That was far too close; we have to be more careful," Kat said. She pulled herself out of the bush, grabbed her backpack and offered Jack her hand to help him out. "So," she whispered, "We were discussing our...gifts." She was brushing the red soil off her clothes as she spoke. "I can heal myself when I get hurt, it used to take a while at first, but it has gotten faster over time."

"I knew it had to be something like that!" Jack said with a small smile. "You *did* hurt your hands on the obstacle course, didn't you?"

"I didn't think anyone noticed that," Kat said quietly, trying not to panic. "See? If I didn't notice you had spotted me, how do we know no one else has noticed? We have to be careful. If we get caught...."

"...we will end up like Ben." Jack finished his cousin's sentence for her. He rubbed at his temples again. His headache would not go away. "We will be fine. My mom has told me not to worry. We have to continue to take the tests as normal and not tell anyone else. We have to make sure we are alone when we speak, and you need to not get hurt in front of people."

The two of them, now as clean as they could get from their hiding spot, rushed to get back to the school and sat in the cafeteria to eat their lunch. As they were eating, they saw Maya walk through the hall. She stopped and glared at them; her fury was as plain as the nose on her face.

"Is there a problem, Maya?" Jack asked her coolly. He put his sandwich down as his hands had started to shake in anger for what she had done to Ben. "Because it looks to me like you are very happy to see us," he smirked. Jack was acting far more confident than he felt but knew that Maya would not say or do anything too bad under the eyes of the lunchtime supervisors and other kids in the room.

Maya seemed unable to speak; she opened her mouth and made a choking sort of snarl, and stormed off. Kat and Jack burst out laughing together. Some of it was relief from surviving the situation they were in earlier; some of it was from scoring a small victory against someone they hated with every core of their beings.

Later that evening, Kat was lying in bed thinking about Ben and her conversation with Jack earlier. She was worried about her test; she had four more nights of sleep to go. *"My mom has told me not to worry."* What did Jack mean by that? She wished she had more chance to speak to him about what her aunt had said to him. Kat trusted Jack, she also had no choice but to go through with her test. She couldn't

63

tell her parents; that could get them into trouble and make them worry. Kat needed to speak to her aunt, she appeared to know far more about what was going on than she did.

Chapter 10 – Kat's Test Day

In the car on the way home, Jack was talking to his aunt about his birthday plans. Kat listened quietly, worrying about the next day. Jack was planning to have a very quiet birthday with just his parents; they were going to watch a movie at the local cinema and have a takeaway when they got home. He was mainly looking forward to his test result party the week after. He hoped Ben would be back by then, but something in his heart told him that Ben would not make it. They pulled up on the side of the road outside his house as usual. Kat's mom reached into the glove compartment and pulled out a card.

"Happy Birthday for tomorrow, Jack. Hope you have a good day," Kat's mom said as she handed him the envelope. Kat looked towards Jack's house, watching and hoping her aunt came to the door.

Kat had not had a chance to speak to her aunt in the run-up to her test day. Thursday had been a busy day at school, her aunt had not been at the door to greet Jack when her mom dropped him off. Kat's test was at ten o'clock on Saturday morning. She spent every waking moment worrying about what would happen. Jack had done his best during the rest of the week at school to reassure her, confident that his mom would be right. Her aunt had never given her son a reason to doubt her, so it was this tiny glimmer of hope that Kat clung to with every fibre of her body. Kat did her best to smile and hugged her cousin tightly as it was time to say goodbye.

"Happy Birthday Jack," she said. She tried to say more, but she couldn't; she felt like she was saying goodbye forever.

"You will be fine. I promise," Jack said. He was worried too, but if she passed, so could he the following week. He put all of his trust in his mom and her certainty that they would be fine. He had to trust her. If he couldn't, then who could he trust? He got out of the car and walked up to his front path. He turned and waved at the door; his father answered and let him in, smiling and waving at the car. Kat waved back, a weight of hopelessness pulling at her chest, as her aunt was, again, not at the door. She could have walked up to the house and asked for her, but not wanting to arouse suspicions, she decided she had to just trust Jack and hope for the best. What happened the next day would be far beyond her control either way.

The following day, Kat woke early again with a heavy feeling in her heart. She did not want this day to start. The red sunrise and clouds that were peeking through the gap in her curtains, made the whole room glow as if it were on fire. Kat wondered distractedly if she could survive a fire but wasn't about to try and find out.

She heard her parents talking in the next room. She knew they were whispering so as not to wake her, but it didn't matter. Nothing mattered now except getting her test completed and that negative result. She got dressed and made her way downstairs, just as her parents had done. It was only seven o'clock, and there had hardly ever been a time where they had all been awake downstairs at that time on a Saturday morning.

"Morning, Sweetheart," her father said as he kissed her on the head. "Ready to smash your test? Was thinking of going out for ice cream afterwards if you feel up to it?"

She nodded, taking her seat at the table next to her mother, who had laid out her cereal as usual. Kat felt sick and didn't want to eat, but the feeling soon passed, and she forced herself to eat the crispy hoops in her bowl.

"You will be fine, Kathryn. I know it's scary; we all were worried when we took our tests. It doesn't hurt much, just a little scratch if you are lucky, it will be over in no time." Her mom was studying her face and looked a little concerned.

"Right, we have to leave the house at nine-thirty to get to the test centre on time. I'm going to check the car over now, before we set off," Dad said. He left Kat and her mom alone to finish their breakfast.

"Mom..." Kat began quietly. "I... erm, need to tell you something."

"You finished with your cereal?" her mom asked. Kat nodded, and her mom removed the bowl. "You don't need to tell me what's bothering you, Sweetheart, come here." She sat down on her chair again, and Kat moved over for a hug. Her mom's warm hands were soothing on the back of her neck. *"I know, Kat,"* her mom's voice echoed inside her head. *"You must not tell anyone, not even Daddy. Don't even say it out loud, ever. I have a deviance too. I can read minds when I am touching people's skin, I can speak to them in their heads too."*

67

Kat pulled away from her mother in shock and stared at her just as her father walked back in, grabbed his coat off the hook and walked back out. He noticed nothing out of the ordinary.

"Typical, it has just started raining," he said with a laugh. "He smiled at the pair of them and headed off back to the car.

Elizabeth looked at her daughter and sighed. She would have to explain a few things to her afterwards when they had more time, but some would have to wait until she was older. She had hoped to alleviate Kat's worries, not make them worse.

"You are going to be okay, please don't worry. I would not send you to the test centre if I couldn't guarantee that you would pass." Liz said. "All you need to know is that you *will* pass today." She gave Kat a slight squeeze on the upper arm, pulled her in for another cuddle, and they went into the living room to watch the television until it was time for them to leave.

Kat was still in shock, her mind was reeling with what she had found out about her mother and realised that she should have gone to her own mother as soon as Jack had told her about his mother. They were sisters after all, it made sense that they could both be Deviants.

The longer they spent in the car on the way to the test centre, the more agitated Kat became. She was desperately trying to keep calm and not to give her secret away. More importantly, she tried not worry that her test would be positive. They finally pulled up at the test centre and made their way to a large, white building with darkened windows. A guard with a gun, dressed all in black, stood outside. He had hard, black eyes and a pointed face; he also had a thick, ugly-looking scar down the left side of his face, going through his eyebrow.

Kat stopped still when she saw him. *They know, she thought,* with her heart racing and panicking slightly. *They are going to take me away.* Her heart was beating hard against her small ribs, and she felt like it was about to break free. She realised her father was speaking and snapped back out of her thoughts, looking at him, crouched down in front of her, looking a little worried.

"Kathryn, are you alright?" he asked quietly. "You look a little pale." He put his hand on her cheek and stroked her face. "There is no need to worry; everyone has to take this test, we will be in and out in a short while, and we can go get some dessert as a treat. Your choice." he said with a smile. He stood up and held out his hand for her to walk together with him into the building. She looked again at the guard but he didn't move.

"Come on, Sweetheart, there is no need to worry." Kat's mom had reached for her hand and held it in both of her own. "I can't wait for dessert," she said with a special smile for her daughter. She hoped that her sister could deliver on her promise with all her heart. Holding her daughter's hand tightly and feeling her give her hand a slight squeeze back, she followed her husband past the armed guard and into the building.

Kat and her mom made their way to a group of chairs in the corner of the empty waiting room. The walls were painted a light, minty green. There was a television in the corner of the room with the day's weather forecast showing. The chairs were old, and the material had been worn on many seats. The cushions were stained on most of them too. The receptionist sat behind a desk near the entrance. She was talking to a man in a white coat with black hair.

"You are going to be fine, Sweetheart. It will all be over soon," Kat's mom said, looking at her daughter. She brushed a strand of Kat's long brown hair from her face and tucked it behind her ear. She could see how nervous she was, and, looking around, she put her hand on Kat's arm and sent calming thoughts to her daughter. She could see her shoulders relax slightly. The ability to manipulate a person's mood had come naturally to Elizabeth over the years. Her powers had matured fully and, as she was a very cautious woman by nature, she could conceal them very well indeed.

She was a girl when she started to see flashes of her sister's thoughts. They were climbing the large apple tree in the family garden when Claire fell from the tree. She had hit her head hard as she fell and had knocked herself out. There was a cut on her forehead that was bleeding. Elizabeth climbed down as fast as she could, shouting her older sister's name, and rushed to her side. She put her hand on her shoulder and shook her hard. Liz's terror at her sister being hurt melted away, and she could see herself, her mother and her father, sitting around the dinner table. In shock, she let go of her sister, and the image disappeared as soon as it had appeared.

Over her childhood, Elizabeth used to sneak up on her sister when she was sleeping and hold her hand to see what she was thinking. She watched her dreams until she fell asleep and would wake up in bed with her sister the following day. After her test results came back negative, she assumed that she was very good at hiding her powers and eventually shared her secret with her sister.

"Kathryn Richards, please make your way through this door, please, and head into room five," the receptionist's voice rang crisp and clear across the waiting room, snapping Elizabeth out of her memories and back into the room with her daughter. She was standing at the doorway, holding it open for her.

Kat stood up and looked at her parents, who remained seated.

"Aren't you coming with me?" she asked them. The fear she had earlier had gone, but she was still confused.

"Everyone who takes the tests has to go through the doors alone, Honey," her father explained. "It is to make sure that nobody other than the person taking the test can affect it. It's a security measure." He stood up and hugged his daughter, "Go on, we will be right here when you come out, just keep thinking of that dessert," he said with a smile.

"Remember, we both love you, Kathryn." Her mother stood up, kissed her on the head and motioned to the door, where the receptionist was still waiting.

"I love you both too," she replied with a dry mouth. Kat's legs had turned to jelly, but she smiled at her parents and walked towards the door, wondering whether or not those would be the last words they said to one another.

Chapter 11 – The Test

The corridor was poorly lit and had numbered doors on both sides. Each entry had a tiny keypad with numbers on it. Security seemed tight. Another guard was at the end of the corridor, also dressed in black and holding a gun. Her footsteps echoed down the hall, and the guard watched her approach. He had a black beard and blue eyes, his face seemed less scary than the guard outside, but he was still a giant of a man to a seven-year-old girl. He was standing outside the door that she was supposed to go through and stopped next to him. He looked at her, smiled and typed a code into the keypad.

The door slid open silently, and a brightly lit room appeared behind it. A chair, similar to that found at the dentist, was in the middle of the room and the man talking to the receptionist was also there. There was even a sink attached to the chair and Kat noticed thin, rectangular holes that ran at intervals along the edges of the chair and wondered what they were for. A smaller chair and a desk with a computer on it were also in the room. The door slid noiselessly back into place behind her, the guard remained outside in the corridor.

"Hello Kathryn, my name is Dr Gibbs. I will be taking your samples this morning, so if you wouldn't mind taking a seat and rolling up a sleeve for me, please, we can get you back outside to your mom and dad as soon as possible."

He seemed pleasant enough to Kat but seemed to be in a bit of a hurry, so she jumped onto the chair, rolling up her sleeve. The doctor sat typing at the computer but stopped once she had sat down, moving beside the chair in the middle of the room where she was sat.

A small table laden with equipment was set up at the side of the chair. Glass phials and a needle were on the table by a little sink. The doctor was double-checking that he had all he needed to complete the tests. Music played from his radio quietly, and he hummed along to the song. "We will start with the blood test first, then finish with the swab."

Kat nodded and looked away when the needle went in. She couldn't watch. But although there was a sharp scratch of pain, the doctor did not see or say anything, so she assumed all was well. He put a plaster over the place he had taken the sample from.

"You may have a little bit of a bruise come up over the next day or two, but you will be fine," Doctor Gibbs said. He then took out the equipment for the swab. Kat then opened her mouth, and he brushed along the inside of her cheeks. He popped the samples in a bag and wrote her name on the front.

"All done, little lady. Well done, you handled that very well," Dr Gibbs said. "Here you go," he gave her a lollipop, stood up and put her samples into a small chute in the corner of the room. He closed the hatch and pressed a button. Kat watched as she saw her sample disappear up the clear plastic pipe. "You are free to leave now."

Kat jumped down off the chair, trying to not appear too anxious and leave too quickly, forcing herself to walk slowly towards the door, she reached for the door handle...

"Hang on a second," the doctor said. Kat froze to the spot, her blood turned to ice in her veins, her heart felt like it would stop any minute. She held her breath. This was it. She had been caught...

"I've just got to press the buzzer to open the door," he said, reaching across his desk in the corner of the room and pressing a green button on the wall. Kat sighed with relief and opened the door onto the corridor.

Kat stepped out into the corridor, hardly daring to believe it was over; the armed guard was still there by the door she came through. He had stepped aside to let her pass but immediately moved back to his post. Kat looked up at him again, he definitely did not seem so scary now the test was complete, she smiled up at him. The guard gave her a small wink and adjusted his position.

She had survived the test; she could leave and go out for dessert with her parents. The fact that she hadn't been caught yet made her feel like laughing and crying at the same time. She continued down the corridor pushed another buzzer to open the door to the waiting room and beamed at her parents. It was over, for now.

Chapter 12 – Results Day

The following week passed Kat by in a blur. She went to school and ate lunch with Jack, who had brought her some birthday cake. She kept her head down and focused on her schoolwork. *It had to be negative. Please let it be negative...* The results from her test were all her brain would allow her to think about.

Jack, however, had done his best to try and distract her, but he too, was preoccupied. Now that he knew that what he called his "big dreams" were real, Jack was doing his best to try and encourage them to keep happening. Every night before bed, he would be thinking of Ben and trying to recall his best friend's face, voice, and smile. His heart ached with the worry of what he would see if he did manage to dream about him and whether he would see him again in person.

Mrs Green had asked him to stay behind after class on Thursday and sat next to him at his group's table. Kat muttered something about meeting him in the car and distractedly grabbed her things and left.

"I know you are worried about Ben, but I am sure he will be back soon," Mrs Green said, with a sad tone to her voice as she sat down. "I have taken his name and picture off his coat peg as I have had to make space for a new starter, but I was wondering whether you would like this." She slid Ben's class picture across the table, and Jack burst into tears. He missed his best friend, and this act of kindness from his teacher struck him hard. Ben was smiling, he looked happy in the photo, his blue eyes sparkled, and his golden hair shone in the light. The school photos had been taken a week before Kat's party, Ben had many happy things to look forward to when this was taken.

"He is your best friend. I know you miss him, you should look after his picture until he gets back, then we can find a new home for it." his teacher said gently. She pulled him into a hug; she would make sure Ben would not be forgotten. She had to hold out hope, not only for Ben but for Jack's sake too. Feeling Jack sobbing into her chest, tears burned the corners of her own eyes. Ben was one of the sweetest children she had ever had the pleasure to teach, and she knew he had been taken away unfairly. The rumours circulating about what happened to Ben amongst the staff at the school had varied. Still, they all started with Maya and her mother reporting him for showing "evidence" of being a Genetic Deviant. She knew, one day, karma would hopefully play out for them.

"Thank you, Miss," Jack said eventually, drying his eyes and moving back from her hug. "I will keep it safe for him." He carefully put the picture in his shirt pocket, and they both stood up. He left the classroom and slowly started making his way to the car. His teacher watched him as he left with a deep sadness in her heart.

Very early the following morning, Kat was awoken by a loud knocking on the front door. She had been awake pretty much all night and was so tired she could now barely keep her eyes open. Her dad, who was already up, getting ready for work, answered it. Kat lay in bed, her heart hammering hard. That had to be her results. She could hear her father talking with the postman; she got out of bed and ran downstairs, making it to the breakfast table just as her dad got there. Her mom was in the middle of buttering some toast and had frozen in mid-air.

The letter came in a thick brown envelope addressed to *The Parents of Kathryn Richards*. Her dad sat down at the table and smiled at her, confidently; her mother had gone a little pale but still forced a smile for her family. Kat could feel her hands shaking; she clasped them together tightly and sat down, waiting as her father opened the envelope.

He took out a booklet and a single-page letter. He started reading the letter. He smiled then put the letter down.

"Negative. What else did we expect?" Kat's father said with a small laugh. Kat relaxed into her chair and breathed a huge sigh of relief. Her mother started laughing, relief visible on her face too and smiling from ear to ear.

"Brilliant, see? Nothing to worry about, Sweetheart." Kat's mom said as she made her way around the table and kissed her daughter's forehead. "All of that worrying for nothing."

Kat felt happy; she knew that she would still have to be very careful, going forward. She would definitely be reported if she was found out and if her power was revealed. She needed to learn more about her deviance but not yet, for now, she was safe. The government tested children at the ages of seven years and fourteen years old, a week after those birthdays. She now had seven years to ensure she would pass again.

"It's Jack's test tomorrow, isn't it?" Kat asked.

"Yes, that's right, at one o'clock", her father answered, standing up and grabbing his keys. "His dad is taking him alone as his mom has a dentist appointment at midday." He grabbed a piece of toast off his wife's plate and stuffed it into his mouth. "I have to go to work now, but I will see you both later." He kissed his wife, then kissed Kat on the head, grabbing his coat as he opened the kitchen door and made his way out to the car. Kat had fallen asleep at the table, her chin resting on her chest, the stresses from the past couple of weeks now vanished.

"Kat, wake up, Sweetie," her mom said gently. "Why don't you take the day off school? I can tell them that you have had your results today and are celebrating a negative result. You can go back to bed if you like?"

"Mmm-okay, Mom," Kat said sleepily. She hugged her mom and made her way upstairs back to bed. The worries from the past couple of weeks had finally left her body; she was free! Somehow, she had managed to get a negative test result, and now all she wanted to do was sleep. Jack would hear that she had tested negative at school and would hopefully not be worried at all now as there was a chance that he could do the same.

Getting in to bed, Kat's train of thought now shifted towards Ben. They had to try and rescue him. She had to speak to her mother, understand her deviance and try and understand her own more too. Knowing that Ben's situation was out of her control and that she could not help him at that very moment, she allowed her mind to finally switch off for the first time in a while and fell into a deep sleep.

Chapter 13 - Jack's Test

Jack was shaken awake by his mother on the morning of his test. He had overslept, and his dad had gone into work earlier that morning for a short meeting.

"Jack, hurry and get ready. Your dad will be home very soon. You need to be ready to leave when he does. Your breakfast is downstairs ready to be eaten, and I have to leave the house myself in ten minutes for my appointment." Jack rubbed his eyes, his hair was sticking up at odd angles too. He groaned but dragged himself out of bed. He had been awake for a while last night and was still pretty tired. He threw on some clothes and made his way downstairs.

"You look nice, mom," Jack said, sleepily as his mom entered the room. He noticed that his mom was wearing a smart, short navy blue dress with matching high heels.

"Thank you, Darling," she said as she hurriedly fastened some golden earrings to her ears. She hated leaving him alone, but she couldn't miss this appointment. "Do not worry about today. It will all go as planned. Aunty Liz phoned last night; Kat passed her test too." She was now sitting at the dining room table applying a bright, red lipstick in a mirror. She glanced at the clock, grabbed her coat and kissed Jack on the head. "Remember, stay calm, and it will be fine. I love you so much."

"I love you too, Mom." Jack waved as his mom passed the window outside the kitchen, and he turned to eat his cereal.

He sat there in silence, trying not to think about his test. He was thinking about Ben again. He had spent a great deal of time trying to encourage a dream about Ben to see if he was alright, but he was unsuccessful. Jack carried his photo wherever he went. He couldn't help feeling responsible for him being taken away; he should have done something, anything. He hoped with all his heart that he was still alive.

Twenty minutes had passed, and Jack's father had still not turned up. Remembering what his mother had said about being ready for when he arrived, he made sure he had his shoes on and ran a comb through his hair. He decided to sit on the front doorstep and wait outside as it was a warm day. The door latch locked behind him as he shut the front door, and he waited. After a short while, he could hear a familiar car engine speeding down the road. It was his father's car.

The sleek, black, government-issued car screeched to a halt outside Jack's home. The driver's window came down, and his dad's face appeared.

"Come on, Jack!" he shouted, "We are going to be late for your test if we don't hurry!" Jack ran down the path and jumped into the front passenger seat, reaching for his seat belt. His father looked a little frazzled. His usually gelled and smooth hair started to stick up slightly at the back from running his hands through it; his brown eyes looked darker too.

"Hi Dad, are you okay?" Jack asked. The car had sped off before Jack had properly clipped in his seatbelt.

"Yeah, I'm fine, Son, the meeting at work ran over. Sorry for being late. You weren't on your own for long, were you? Your mother's dental appointment couldn't have landed on a worse day."

"Not too long, I was fine," Jack replied. He noted that his dad was driving pretty fast along the roads, despite being so busy. His dad continued to speed along the streets, weaving in and out of traffic, he seemed preoccupied, but they eventually managed to make it to the test centre, somehow making it there with five minutes to spare.

They walked quickly towards the white building with darkened windows. The guard standing at his post by the entrance spotted Jack's father, jumped to attention and saluted him.

"Captain Roberts, Sir!" he said as he brought his hand down and reached for the door handle.

"Thank you, as you were," Jack's dad replied. He put his hand on Jack's shoulder and guided him into the waiting room. He walked to the receptionist's desk to check-in, and Jack took a seat.

"Do you know that man, Dad?" Jack asked.

"Not really, but he knows me from work. I was a soldier too, a long time ago," his dad explained. Jack nodded and settled into the chair, looking around at the posters on the wall.

The truth was, Captain Martin Roberts was a highly decorated soldier, awarded medals for bravery in a war fought many years ago. He was injured, and his knee was damaged; he had been fighting in a war against a far-off nation that wanted to help Deviants. They promoted the idea that their powers could be used for good, that not all of them were bad or destructive and that they could help humanity advance, benefitting from them. The nation was ultimately destroyed; no other nation or region tried to support the Deviants after that. It was an international agreement that all countries would actively search for them and expose them. However, some governments did utilise them if their powers were beneficial, but that was not always public knowledge, it varied from country to country.

A door had opened, the receptionist came through it; she smiled at Jack as he looked up.

"Jack Roberts, you can go in now, look for room number five," she said; she held the door open for him, he stood up. He looked at his father, who put his hand on his shoulder and smiled at him.

"Go get 'em, Son. See you in a short while." He gave Jack's shoulder a slight squeeze and ruffled his hair a little. Jack decided that worrying about the test would no longer do any good and walked calmly across the waiting room. If it turned out to be negative, he would carry on, as usual, keep his dreams a secret as best as he could, and that would be the end of it. If he turned out to be positive, he would possibly end up where Ben was and hopefully find him or help him somehow. In his seven-year-old eyes, it was now a win-win situation.

He walked along the corridor and spotted a second armed guard who opened the door to the testing room and held the door open for him.

"Thank you," Jack said quietly; his mouth had suddenly gone dry, he was finding it hard to speak. The doctor in the room was sitting at his desk in the corner; he turned around smiling at Jack.

"Hello there, Jack. How's your father doing?" He moved towards Jack and motioned for him to take a seat in the examination chair in the centre of the room.

"Good, thanks, he's in the waiting room at the minute," Jack replied.

"Ah, of course, he is," the doctor said with a chuckle. "Glad to hear it. Tell him I asked about him, won't you?"

"Sure," said Jack. He was a little unsettled by how many people seemed to know his father and a bit uneasy about how little he seemed to know about him himself. Jack climbed into the chair, and the doctor moved towards the small table that held the equipment he would be using.

"Right, blood test first then," he said, more to himself than to Jack. Noting that Jack had a cast on his right arm, he rolled up Jack's left sleeve and tied a tourniquet around his arm above the elbow. Jack braced himself; he had never had a blood test before and tensed up his arm. The sharp pain he felt when the needle punctured his skin caused him to flex his arm involuntarily, taking the needle out of his skin and causing the doctor to drop it. Jack held his arm out once more and turned away from the doctor. The vial made a tinkling sound as it hit the floor and smashed. The doctor looked startled.

"I am so sorry…" began Jack. "It made me jump. It hurt me." He was starting to panic a little. What if he wasn't allowed to have the test retaken?

"Don't worry. I can try again; just please be still. We aren't usually allowed to make a second attempt and we are supposed to report any failed attempts. But

I will try again, just for you," the doctor said, smiling and winking.

Truthfully, he valued his job at the testing facility; he had bills and a family to provide for. If he were to report the failed attempt to his superiors, they would be bound by law to investigate the person who was being tested and their immediate family. Explaining to Captain Roberts that he would have to be investigated, given his reputation among the higher-ranking officials in the government, would not be an option that would end with a positive outcome for the doctor. He would just say he dropped the vial and had to use another.

Jack's mind was reeling; he was doing his best to follow his mother's advice and remain calm. He took a few deep breaths and sat back, once again, in the chair. He held out his arm and continued to take deep breaths.

"I'm alright now," Jack said. "I am so sorry."

"Right, please hold still. We cannot afford to lose another vial. It will be a short, sharp scratch but will be over before you know it. Just listen to this music if it helps." The doctor walked over to his desk and turned on his radio. Music played and drifted through the room. Jack focused on it, looking away from his arm and the needle.

"There we go, great stuff." The doctor was pleased that he had finally managed to get a sample of Jack's blood and also took the swab with no trouble whatsoever. He sealed the test samples in a plastic bag and wrote some details on its front. He walked over to the small chute in the corner of the room and placed them inside. Shutting the hatch, he pressed a button next to it, Jack watched his samples go up through the ceiling. "You are free to go now, Jack. Take a lollipop from off my desk on your way out." Jack got up from his chair, and the pair of them walked to the doctor's desk. He chose a green lollipop from the plastic dish and walked to the door. The doctor pressed a button, the door opened, and the guard was standing in the doorway looking down at him.

Jack walked straight past the guard, down the dimly lit corridor and pressed the button at the end of the hallway to regain access to the waiting room. Opening the door, he looked around for his father. He was not in the waiting room. Jack was confused for a moment. He wandered over to where he was sitting and found nothing; he turned on the spot and headed towards the receptionist. Maybe she had seen something? She was not there either.

"I have to wait for my son!" Jack heard his father's raised voice coming from outside. He left the waiting room and followed the sound of his father's shouting. "I will be there as soon as I can. You will just have to wait." Jack found his father on the phone, pacing up and down the car park next to his car. He spotted his son and waved, trying to smile. Jack walked over to him in time just to hear him say, "I will be there; I will drop him off and come straight back over." He pressed a button on his phone and put it in his pocket with a sigh.

"Hi, Dad," Jack said. "Is everything alright?" He noticed that his dad was sweating and looking worried.

"Hey, how was your test? Did it go well?" Captain Roberts asked his son, ignoring his question. "I'm sorry, I have to drop you back off home and head straight back to work. The meeting from this morning did not finish well, and I must go back and finish it as soon as you are home. I really am so sorry I can't stay and celebrate your test being over, we can do something together later when I get back."

"Okay, no problem." Jack replied, a little disappointed. "Will Mom be back when we get home?" he asked. He didn't feel much like spending time alone after his test. Despite his mother's reassurances, he was still shaken and slightly worried about his results. He was starting to feel an all too familiar headache creep in across his temple and needed not to have his father around when it kicked in properly. It was his first headache in a while, and whilst he did not enjoy having them, he hoped he could use it to try and see where Ben was.

"She should be by then. It was only a dental appointment, just a follow up from some treatment she had last week, so she should beat us home," his father replied. He unlocked the car, and they both got inside. Jack's father was again driving at a breakneck speed.

"Dad, can you slow down a little, please?" Jack asked. He was feeling a little sick, and his headache was getting worse.

"Sorry, Son, I can't," he replied, glancing across at the time on the dashboard. "I have to get back for that meeting. I must be there…."

Suddenly, with the sound of some costly tyres skidding and screeching and the sickening sound of metal being crumpled, the car had spun off the road on a tight corner and hit a large tree. The impact mainly hit the driver's side of the vehicle, but Jack had bumped his forehead, and it was bleeding a lot. He looked at his father, who was also bleeding. The tree had smashed into his father's car door and pushed metal into his leg; he had been knocked unconscious.

Jack felt fuzzy, his headache had significantly worsened, and all he wanted to do was sleep. Everything was starting to go dark; he felt heavy, he closed his eyes and he also fell unconscious.

Chapter 14 – Answers

Jack was in a very plain, white room. He was wearing dark blue pyjamas and was lying on a hard bed. There were no windows and only a table with a glass of water on it to keep him company. He sat up and rubbed his eyes; he was wearing glasses. His stomach did a somersault. He had managed to get into a "big dream" this was Ben!

He reached out and picked up the glass. Jack noticed that his hands were bruised and had puncture marks in his skin on the back of his hand. It hurt for him to move too much, but he managed to drink some water. It tasted funny, but it would have to do. He looked around the room. The door was made from heavy metal and had a hatch in its middle and a small window above it, looking out onto a corridor.

He heard people talking and footsteps heading in his direction. He stood up and painfully shuffled to the hatch, hoping to catch a glimpse of the people passing by. They stopped outside his door; he heard the jangle of a set of keys.

"Step away from the door, Phillips, and turn to face away from the door," said a deep voice. "Put your hands above your head." Jack felt Ben's pain as he did as he was told. He turned and stepped away, trying to raise his arms as directed. His entire body hurt from the various tests he had been subjected to, Jack felt every single bit of his agony.

The door clicked open, and two burly armed guards entered the room. One grabbed Ben's arms roughly and handcuffed them together; the other stood by the door.

"Going to show us what you can do today, Phillips?" the second guard mocked. Both men were huge, especially to a child. "We have a lovely day planned for you."

Jack felt utterly helpless as he was marched out of the room, watching through Ben's eyes, feeling his pain and worries. They made their way down a corridor, turning left along a second corridor to a brightly lit room with a flat, metal bed with holes in it. He noticed that there were leather straps on it, and he knew Ben had spotted it too. He felt Ben's heart hammering and he stopped walking.

"Move it, Phillips, get on the bed," the first guard said. "The doctor will be in here any minute." He felt the guard shove him from behind, and he started moving again. The door opened, and a third, very short, man entered the room. He wore a white coat and thick-rimmed glasses, making his brown eyes look insect-like and disproportionately big. He had a slight hunch in his back from many years pouring over research papers and books. He was very respected in his field of research, which involved encouraging dormant powers within Genetic Deviants to show themselves.

The guards picked Ben up and strapped him to the table and removed his glasses. The room had now gone blurry at the edges and greatly limited the field of vision he had. He tried to free himself, but he was too weak, and the straps were too tight.

"Afternoon all," the doctor said as he walked to the desk in the room. He had a slight squeak in his

voice and an accent Jack did not know, "Ben, my name is Doctor Petrov and today we will be testing to see if your power is elemental. We will first try water, then maybe electricity... it all depends on how we get on," he said with a snigger. "Gentlemen," he said, addressing the guards that had escorted Ben to the room, "I will send for you when I am finished. Thank you."

The two guards left, and Ben was now alone with this doctor preparing to hurt him, just like the other doctors before him.

"I don't have power, Doctor. I shouldn't be here. I'm only six years old, I haven't even had my test yet. That girl, Maya, lied...." Ben said, but the doctor cut him off.

"I have been told your results were positive, so until I am told otherwise, all I am concerned with, is running my tests and doing my job. So please, it will be easier for us both if you just cooperate. It may hurt, but as soon as you show your deviance, the sooner we can decide if you are worth anything to us."

"Please, don't do this...." Ben was starting to feel desperate. Jack was horrified; he didn't know how much more of this he could watch. He needed to help Ben by getting him out of wherever he was held. He tried to look around for anything that could help him identify where he was being kept.

The bed was raised a little higher for the doctor's comfort. The edges were all raised higher than Ben's head, and with a jolt of fear, he realised that he was in what would look like a fish tank. The doctor was connecting machines to him. Another canular with an IV drip was attached to his hand, metal discs were

90

placed on his chest and head. He had been connected to a heart monitor, and the beep-beep-beep of the heart machine started to speed up as Ben's state of panic increased.

"Right, let's begin, shall we?" the doctor said. He had a horrible look on his face that indicated that he would enjoy what he was about to do. He had a computer screen next to the bed, and he wheeled his chair from his desk to observe and take notes. He touched the computer screen a couple of times, Ben was doing his very best to try and break free, but he was so exhausted. He had already been here for around two weeks, and he was slowly starting to believe that he would never leave this place.

Although he couldn't read his best friend's thoughts, Jack was experiencing everything as Ben himself was experiencing it. It was impossible to explain it, but he could sort of feel his best friend's mood and felt he was close to giving up altogether. He willed with all his strength that Ben could feel him too and tried to think positive things to try and communicate to Ben that he was not alone.

Ben gasped as he started to feel cold water underneath him on the table. What little warmth he had, left his body almost immediately. His teeth began to chatter as goosebumps appeared, almost painfully all over his body. The water did not stop rising, and it soon started filling his ears. The doctor studied Ben's reactions and wrote everything he observed into his notebook.

"Please," Ben said, in a quiet voice, "You don't have to do this; just rerun my blood test. It will be negative." He was ignored by the doctor. He

wondered how many more painful and horrific tests he would have to endure before he either died or they decided that he was not a deviant after all.

As the water covered his eyes, leaving his mouth and nose almost free if he tilted his head, he thought of his parents, thought of Kat, and he thought of his best friend, Jack. He missed his birthday... Had he missed his results party too? He was losing track of days now and finding it harder and harder to keep breathing above the water. Eventually, the water went up to his nose and down his throat, drowning him.

"Ben!" screamed Jack in his head. "You have to hold on...." Jack was still observing everything and feeling everything Ben was going through. Once Ben had passed out and was slowly drowning, he couldn't see any more but could still hear and feel what was happening to his best friend. Knowing that Ben was still alive, but barely. He could hear a faint beeping from the machine measuring his heart rate, which was getting slower and slower. Ben's body had started twitching, fighting to breathe but unable to. Eventually, it stopped, and so did the beeping. Jack saw nothing but darkness for a while.

A painful, needle-like shockwave ran through Ben's body, and he was alive again. Ben arched his back and gasped, drawing in cool air and spitting up water. He was shaking from the cold. It appeared that he had just been electrocuted back to life. Close to death, coughing and spluttering to try and get his breath back, Ben felt terrible; he had had enough, he wanted to die. He didn't know what else they could do to him without starting to detach body parts. He shuddered and did his best to stay calm. He looked up at the doctor, who had barely moved. Ben had just died, his end wouldn't be so bad, he thought...

Jack was horrified. Not only had he just felt his best friend die, but he was also not able to leave his dream. He wondered why he hadn't woken up and was starting to worry that he was stuck here watching Ben being tortured to death and not be able to do anything to stop it.

"So, no power observed..." the doctor said out loud as he wrote some notes down into his book. "Let us go again, shall we? Just in case." He pressed a few more buttons onto the computer screen next to the bed, and the water that had drained whilst Ben was being resuscitated, was slowly starting to fill the tank again. Ben felt heavy as if his entire body was made from lead, and he just stared at the ceiling. The icy water slowly started to creep around his body again, and Ben just lay there. He realised that there was no use in pleading with this doctor; he would just have to obey his orders.

On the other hand, Jack used every single ounce of mental strength to will Ben to keep fighting.

"Come on, Ben, we need you!" he was shouting, hoping Ben would hear him. "I need you," he added quietly. "Please, don't give up. I will get you out of there, I promise!"

The water had covered Ben's eyes again, and he didn't even fight to keep his mouth or nose above it this time. He just lay there, closed his eyes and let himself drown again.

"NOOO!" shouted Jack as he could no longer see anything again; he felt a surge of raw emotion course through him. He tried to guide it through to Ben. The

93

beeping had stopped, and the sharp needle-like pain had coursed through Ben's body again. This time, however, Ben did not wake. The electricity crashed through Ben's body a second time, still, no response from Ben. Jack could not bear to see his best friend die again, to not be at his side in person and feel him die thinking he was alone. A longer, more painful shock blitzed through Ben's body once more, and Ben opened his eyes. Among the coughing and spluttering of Ben, breathing and awake once more, Jack was in shock. He was so happy that Ben was alive again but dismayed as it meant the torture would carry on. Ben had given up now, he was ready for the torture to end.

With every extra fibre of thought he could muster, Jack tried to send Ben a message of hope and to stay strong. Ben tensed, and Jack felt his emotions change. Luckily, the doctor moved away to his desk and could be heard opening some sort of food packaging and eating loudly.

"Jack?" Ben said weakly under his breath. Jack felt a small flame of hope light up in Ben's heart. He pushed as hard as he could to make his thoughts felt by the small boy who had endured so much over the last few weeks. "I'm sorry, Jack, I can't fight much longer, but I will try. Please send help if you can hear me."

Jack was trying to send a message back to Ben, but Ben couldn't place where it was coming from, he could feel his presence, however, which was something. He wasn't alone now and he knew it. He would fight for as long as his little body could hold out.

The doctor came back and took his seat next to the bed again. Picking food out of his teeth distractedly.

"Third time is the charm, they say," he said with a chuckle. The little bit of hope that Jack held in his heart turned to a cold fury towards this evil man. He wasn't sure how many more times his six-year-old friend could die and keep coming back. He felt the water start seeping in around Ben's body once more, and then Jack heard a voice. His mother's voice, calling his name.

"Bye Ben, just keep holding on," Jack said as his mother's voice got louder and his surroundings started to fade. He sent one last push of hope towards his best friend, hoping he felt it.

Chapter 15 – Revelations

"Jack," Jack's mother was standing over him, her hand on his arm, looking exhausted and worried. "Can you hear me?"

Jack and his father's car crash had been seen by other motorists and reported immediately to the emergency services.

Jack had been out cold for a couple of hours and had just started to show signs of coming round. He had sustained a deep cut on his forehead that had been stitched up and a couple of bruises. His father, however, had managed to get his right leg impaled by metal from the car and had broken his right arm. He had also lost a lot of blood due to him hitting his head and had cuts and grazes along his right side from the broken windows. He was currently in a medically induced coma from his injuries but was expected to be woken up soon.

Jack had managed to pull himself out of his connection with Ben. He was utterly horrified at what he had witnessed and was scared that there were people in the world willing to put children through such torture. Aware that he was somewhere other than his bed and that his mother was nearby, he was not prepared to wake up just yet. He lay still with his eyes shut to gather his thoughts. He could feel the helpless anxiety wrap itself around his heart at the thought that Ben may be murdered again and not wake up this time.

He would have to tell his mother and Kat what was going on with Ben. They all had to try and do something to get him out. He didn't know how much more torture his best friend could endure.

Jack felt that his deviance had seemed to change a little too; he was relieved that Ben somehow managed to feel that he was there. Maybe he was getting better at using his gift? Jack felt his mother take his hand and decided to slowly open his eyes. He was in a hospital bed, his mother was sitting in a chair next to the bed, a doctor was standing nearby, observing him.

"Mom, what happened?" Jack murmured as he realised how sore his throat was. He was very thirsty too, which made speaking difficult.

"Oh Jack, I was so worried I was going to lose you," his mom said; she started crying with relief at the sound of his voice. "You and your father have been in an accident. You are going to be alright, your father should be too, all being well. He is still asleep at the moment. You hit your head pretty hard and may have a bit of concussion, but thankfully nothing much worse than that."

"How's Dad?" he asked croakily. "Is he going to be okay?" He reached for a clear plastic jug full of water and a cup on the bedside table. His mother stood up and poured him a drink of water, holding the cup up to his mouth. The cool water soothed his throat and made it easier to speak.

"He has damaged his leg. The doctors pulled some large pieces of metal out from around his knee and he may have to use a walking stick from now on. If he can walk on it again at all. He had to have a blood transfusion as he lost so much blood. He nearly died.

The doctors are keeping him asleep for a few days so he can recover and he will need an operation on his leg, but he'll be alright," his mother explained. "I am so glad you are awake."

The doctor moved to the other side of Jack's bed and started running tests to see how he was doing. He took his temperature, measured his blood pressure and checked his stats on the machine that had been hooked up to him. He seemed happy with the results and added them to his notes on the clipboard that he was holding.

"Okay, Jack, how are you feeling?" he asked. "Any soreness or pain anywhere?" He smiled and flashed a light into his eyes to test his responsiveness.

"Erm, no, I feel fine," said Jack. "He raised his hand to the place where he cut his head and gently ran his fingers over the stitches.

"That's good then. We gave you some pain medication to help you out a little bit. That is a pretty nasty cut on your head, it will take a little time to heal, but you will have a cool looking scar once it is healed, though." The doctor patted him reassuringly on the arm and looked up to Jack's mother, "We are looking to let Jack go home tomorrow, but if there is anything else you need in the meantime, Mrs Roberts, please do not hesitate to press the call button."

"Thank you very much, Doctor," she replied. "We do appreciate everything you have done for us. If you could let us know as soon as anything changes with my husband, we would be so grateful."

"I am headed over to Captain Roberts's room straight from here, don't worry," he said reassuringly. "Your husband is under the finest medical care this country has to offer. The moment his condition changes, you will be the very first to know."

He headed to the door and left the two of them alone in their private room. Jack tried to sit up more and looked at his mother's tired face. She was still wearing the makeup she had put on earlier that day and had been crying a lot as she had tracks of mascara that had run down her cheeks. He was just about to start telling her about Ben when she suddenly leaned forward, smoothing his sheets around him and whispered, in the very smallest of breaths:

"Not here, Sweetheart, tell me at home. It's too dangerous. They are listening." She made him lean forward and plumped up his pillows too, "There we go, Sweetheart," she said in her normal voice, "Is that better?"

"Yes, thanks, Mom," he replied. He was confused and even more scared now. Every minute he was lying in the hospital was another minute that his best friend was alone and hurting, maybe even dead. He lay back on the pillows and looked up at the ceiling, he could feel hot tears prick the corners of his eyes, and he willed himself not to cry. His mom put her hand on his and rested her head on her arm. She fell asleep in minutes. He continued to stare at the ceiling and eventually fell asleep too.

Jack was woken up by the doctor and nurse coming into his room the following day. They had come to check him over before being discharged and ran a few final tests. His mother was not there, but her coat and bag were still on the chair next to his bed.

"Good morning, Jack," the doctor said cheerily. "How are you feeling today?" He was in the process of taking Jack's blood pressure, and the nurse was checking his temperature at the same time.

"I'm feeling better today, thanks," Jack replied. "Where's my mom?"

"She's gone over to see your dad, he is still asleep, but she wanted to see him before they take him down to operate on his leg. He has some metal wedged behind his kneecap and a shard of it deep inside his thigh. He will be fine, try not to worry. It's nothing we can't fix." The doctor explained reassuringly. "Your mom should be back real soon, your blood pressure is fine, and you don't appear to have suffered any long-lasting damage from the crash. You will have a little scar on your head, but that should be it."

The nurse left and returned with some toast and a glass of juice on a tray. She smiled at him, her blue eyes twinkled, and a natural maternal warmth came from her.

"Would you like me to put the television on for you whilst you wait for your mom?" she asked. "Here we go," she said, grabbing the remote from the bedside table and turning on a channel. "My little boy likes this cartoon. Maybe you will too." She moved to the window, opened the curtains and pushed the window open as far as it would go. Then she left the room. The doctor stood at the end of Jack's bed, writing notes on his clipboard.

"Right, you are all clear to leave Jack. As soon as your mom gets back, you are free to go. If you do have any headaches or vision changes, just let us know, and we will do our very best to help." The doctor then left the room, and Jack lay on the bed and stared at the television.

After a short while, Jack sat up and rubbed his eyes. He felt uneasy, unable to shake away the memories of what he had seen in his dream the day before and was in desperate need to speak to his mom. He looked around the room. *"They are listening."* What did his mom mean by that? He couldn't see anything out of the ordinary. Maybe she was referring to the doctors?

He rolled onto his side and opened his bedside cabinet. It had some of his clothes inside, all folded up neatly. He decided that he had better get ready to leave as soon as his mom came back, so they could get home as quickly as possible. He pulled out his clothes and changed.

He heard the sound of high heels on a cold hard floor echoing down the corridor, getting closer with every step. They belonged to his mom. She opened the door and smiled.

"You are all ready to go?" she asked. "I saw the doctor at reception, and he said he has discharged you, so we are free to go home. Your dad is about to have his surgery, though. He will be here for a few days longer still."

She grabbed her coat and bag, held out her hand, and the two of them walked together out of the hospital and into the car park. They got into the car and headed home. Jack's mom turned on the radio, and some music played to fill the silence. After a couple of minutes, there was an interruption in the music, a news broadcast started.

Another person has tested positive for genetic deviations this week. She is fourteen years old and called Sarah Watson, living in the South. She is five feet, four inches tall, with blonde hair and blue eyes. She was last seen wearing a grey tracksuit and running shoes, carrying a large black backpack. It appears she can manipulate water, which could prove extremely useful for the planet as far as we know. However, she has decided not to cooperate with the Government. She attacked the officers that went to her house to escort her for more tests, by causing all the water in their bodies to evaporate, killing them instantly. She is on the run, do not approach her. Anyone with information about her whereabouts, please call the number we will read out at the end of this report. Remember, the law states that "anyone harbouring or protecting a known Deviant will be arrested...".

"That's enough of the radio, I think," said Jack's mom. "Are you alright, Honey?" Jack had been staring out of the window for the entire journey, miles away in his own thoughts. He was still unsure if they could speak freely yet and was worried about Ben. "Jack?" his mother said again. She pulled the car over on a deserted road. They were in the countryside, red, barren fields on either side of the road and large trees shading where they had parked. Jack looked at his mom. She put her fingers to her lips and said: "You look a little pale, want some fresh air?"

"Yes, that might help. I just feel a little sick, that's all," Jack replied, catching on with what his mom was trying to do. "A short walk might help me feel better."

They both got out of the car and walked a short stretch down the road. It was a warm day, and the sky was clear, birds could be heard in the trees above, and a light breeze rustled the leaves.

102

"Okay, Jack, we have a very short time here that we can talk. I doubt we can be overheard here. You just need to know a couple of things. The house is no longer safe to speak. Your dad works for the government, and for some reason, they do not trust any of their employees anymore. We have to assume that we are bugged, I cannot be a hundred per cent sure, but it is best to remain cautious. That also may extend to our cars, your aunt's house and maybe school too. They are most likely already listening in on the hospitals. You just heard yourself on the radio that another deviant has been discovered. It isn't safe for us. What is it that you need to tell me? Did you see Ben?" she asked.

Jack explained his dream as accurately and quickly as possible, feeling even more scared now. He told his mother how he managed to send his feelings to Ben and that Ben could feel it too as he spoke out loud to him. Jack started crying. He felt helpless. They needed to help him. His mom pulled him into a long hug.

"You say the doctor's name was Petrov?" his mother asked. She looked very concerned and had her hand covering her mouth. She had listened to his every word without interruption.

"Yes, do you know him?" Jack asked. "He was killing Ben, Mom. I couldn't do a thing. He could be dead now."

"I will do my best to find out what is going on with Ben, Honey. Now that you have told me what you have seen and given me a name, I have a friend who might be able to help me," she said. "We need to get back to the car now. I know it's terrible, but please try not to worry. Things will be okay. I have seen a few flashes of things that could happen, but the trouble with my power is that what I see is subject to change, so I take what I see with a pinch of salt. It is not always set in stone that what I see will happen for sure as too many variables are always affecting different things."

They got back into the car and continued the rest of their drive in silence. When they arrived back home, Jack went up to his room. He felt better for finally speaking to his mom but would not rest easy until he knew Ben was safe. He wanted to talk to Kat. He hadn't seen her for a couple of days and knew she would probably be worried. Jack felt that she needed warning about what his mother had told him. He stayed in his room for the rest of the day, only coming down when dinner was ready and eating it with his mom. They watched a movie together in the living room, then they went to bed.

The days rolled by slowly. They consisted of Jack and his mom travelling to the hospital to sit at his dad's side all day whilst he was still sleeping. His operation had gone well, but his dad would have to work very hard if he wanted to walk again. They travelled home each day, ate dinner then went to bed. Neither of them spoke much about anything important.

Jack spent any other free time in his room trying to get to grips with his power, which was difficult as he couldn't speak to his mom and her power was different to his, so she would not be able to help much. He found that he had to try and teach himself how to control his power without knowing what to do or how to go about doing it.

Chapter 16 – Results

Saturday eventually made its way around; Jack was lying in bed awake, waiting for the sound of the letterbox that marked his test results arriving. His party had, naturally been cancelled due to the crash. He did not feel like partying anyway with Ben not being around to help him celebrate.

Jack heard the phone ringing downstairs, he sat up and stretched, rubbing his eyes. His mother picked up the phone and spoke to someone. After a bit of chatter, he heard her say goodbye, so he slowly made his way downstairs.

The letterbox rattled as he passed the front door, and he stopped to pick up the letters that had fallen at his feet. He looked at the one marked for his parents that had a government seal on the postmark, put it on the top of the pile and made his way into the kitchen, where his mom sat with a cup of coffee. He stood next to her and waited, his heart rattling against his ribs.

"Good morning! Let's get this over with, shall we?" Jack's mom said as he handed her the letters. She opened the one Jack had put on top first, her hands shaking a little. She skimmed the letter and let out a massive sigh of relief. "It's negative, Jack," Claire said with a smile spreading across her tired face. She stood up and gave her son a tight hug. It was over, for now. Relief washed over her; they had managed to prevent both Jack and Kat from being taken away. Claire needed to share the news with her sister, kissing Jack on the head, she picked up the phone.

Jack's mom arranged to have Liz and Kat over for dinner that evening to celebrate the good news. Jack had spoken to his mom earlier in the week about not having a results party. With Ben not being around and his dad in hospital still, he didn't feel like seeing anyone, but having his aunt and cousin over for dinner would be more manageable.

Chapter 17 – Future Plans

Jack and his mother prepared dinner for Kat and Liz for over an hour before they arrived. They had a homemade chicken pie with apple crumble for dessert. Claire knew that they would have to be very careful with how they handled their situation going forward now and had been thinking about it all afternoon.

The doorbell rang, and she made her way to the door to let them in. It was a cold, blustery day, and leaves blew in with the two guests.

"Hello, Aunty Claire!" Kat said with a smile. "Where's Jack?" She took off her coat and gave it to her aunt to hang up as the hooks were too high for her to reach.

"He's in the kitchen, Sweetheart. Help yourself to a drink; dinner will be ready shortly," Claire replied. She looked at her sister and smiled, pulling her into a tight hug, Liz put her hand on her sister's neck again, and for a moment, they stood there. Claire quickly thought a message to her sister:

"Our houses may be compromised. Let Kat know. The kids' school and our cars could be bugged too. Ben is in trouble and is being tortured. You need to read Jack's mind to see if you can see any details that can help us get him out."

"How are you doing, Liz?" she said out loud. "It has been a while since we had you over for dinner, John not able to make it?"

"No, he's not been feeling well, so he has decided to stay at home and watch the football match. He sends his congratulations to you both, though," Liz replied. She had an apprehensive look on her face, but she had managed to recover quickly from the news she had just received from her sister, to be able to respond with enough speed that if anyone *were* listening in, they would not have noticed.

The two sisters made their way into the kitchen, where their children sat, chatting away. They sat there for a while until Liz passed a written message to Jack, it said:

Do not read this out loud. Aunty Claire can read minds; when she holds your hand during dinner, let her see everything you saw in your dream. She may see something that can help Ben get rescued.

Claire watched him read the note and then locked eye contact with him. He nodded, and she took the piece of paper away, holding it over the gas stove, so it caught fire and dropped it into the sink to be destroyed without a trace. She then dished their food out onto plates and handed them out around the table. His aunt put her hand on his shoulder and smiled at him.

"Dig in everyone, hope you enjoy it," Liz said with a smile. "And thank you for coming, Kat and Liz. It means a lot to us that you could come over and celebrate Jack's test result with us."

"It's our pleasure," said Claire with a smile. She had sat next to Jack at the table, who had been pretty quiet all day.

"Are you okay, Jack?" Kat asked; she was wearing a red dress and a matching bow in her long brown hair. "The cut on your head looks painful," she added, in-between mouthfuls of mashed potato.

"I'm okay, Kat, just a little tired," he replied. He did not feel like eating and felt a little apprehensive about his aunt reading his mind. "How was school this week?" He had missed the entire week from school with special permission from the headteacher. They had generously allowed him to take some time off to recover, to spend time with his dad and had completely understood when his mom had explained the situation to them.

"It was fine. You haven't missed much. I have brought over what you have missed so far, as Mrs Green gave me extra copies of our classwork for you to have a look at." Kat said, shovelling the last of the food into her mouth. "She said that if you are struggling with it, just let her know when you go back, and she will run through it with you. She also said that she understands that you have a lot going on right now, so she will help you catch up when you come back if you don't get to look at it. I can try to help you too if you like?" She burped loudly, then giggled. "Sorry, Aunty Liz, that food was amazing, thank you."

"That is a lovely offer, thank you, Kat," her aunt said, smiling. "We can have you over for a sleepover at some point and work through it together, maybe get some pizza too?" she said with a smile. Liz gave Claire the nod, and her sister placed her hand on the back of Jack's wrist as Claire started to noisily collect the plates and start serving up dessert and fresh drinks.

"Okay, Jack, show me everything," his aunt whispered. They both closed their eyes, Jack replayed everything in as much detail as he remembered. He heard his aunt gasp when she saw what happened to Ben. He felt her hand tighten on his arm. He could

110

hear her voice in his head after he had finished showing her what he had witnessed.

"Thanks, Jack. I cannot believe what that poor boy is suffering through and you, having to witness that! Your mother and I will do what we can to help him. I don't know how much she has told you, but we know a couple of people who may be able to rescue him. The information you have provided will help us locate him faster. If you have any more of these dreams, you must let me or your mom know. They are invaluable to us; they help us more than you realise. I know you feel helpless and pretty low right now, but believe me, when I say, this will help him. Just keep that flame burning that you will see Ben again." She then sent him some calming thoughts and helped ease his worries. It helped, she saw his face relax slightly and his shoulders lowered.

"Here we go, guys, apple crumble!" Jack's mom said with a flourish. "We made it from scratch, didn't we, Jack?" She smiled and placed a large jug of hot custard in the middle of the table. "There's ice cream in the freezer if you would rather not have custard," she said to Kat, smiling.

"We will need to go out for a bit to walk this off, I think," Liz said, looking at her sister. "We can take our car, and I'll drive. I know a lovely spot, just outside the town."

"Sounds like a great idea," agreed Claire. As soon as their bellies were full, they all got ready to leave. It had started raining, but that was not going to discourage Liz from taking them all out. She knew a secluded spot where they would not be overheard and could talk freely. They would be able to try and put

111

together a plan to get Jack and Kat through to their fourteenth birthdays and pass their second Genetic Deviation tests, it would be complicated, but they would find a way. Claire had foreseen it.

Part 2

Chapter 18 – Catch Up

Almost seven years had gone by since Kat and Jack discovered that they were Deviants, hiding from the government. They were doing everything they could to avoid being detected and reported. Their deviances are all hidden for the moment. Kat's mom, Elizabeth, is always adamant about ensuring that Kat has a week off school during every flu season to show that she can get ill, just like the other children in her class. She also made sure to keep her off school when the chickenpox went around her class, as to not arouse suspicion. Kat can completely heal herself and, over the last few years, it had become almost instantaneous.

Jack's gift, however, is far more challenging to cover up. The sisters decided that it was best not to tell anyone else about what they were capable of, so they decided to keep both Jack and Kat's fathers in the dark. This mainly stemmed from Jack's father working with the government and was of a rank where he would be obligated to report even his own family, if they were known to be Deviants. He would also most likely be punished for not knowing about it sooner, that is, if he was to be believed that he had only recently found out. In truth, the actual consequences were unknown, as it was unheard of for deviants to still be undiscovered or reported at adulthood like the sisters were.

As Jack's power had started to change and develop, he realised that his dreams of seeing what he did all began with him suffering a headache beforehand. With these headaches, he had to use pain medication given to him by the doctor to keep them at bay. The doctor was a friend of his mother, and he was able to prescribe Jack medication without Jack giving away his powers. No blood tests were taken as his GD test result was negative, and he was not being investigated. It also helped that the doctor knew his father, who commanded respect for him and his family. The doctor took Jack and his mother at their words and didn't ask too many questions.

Jack discovered that, if he didn't let the pain take over, he didn't slip into any of his dreams. The only time he didn't take the pain medication was when his father was working away from home. That way, if he woke up screaming with his pain, only his mother would hear. They still had to be careful with what was said in the house, just to be on the safe side, but they had developed ways of communication that would go unheard and undetected if they were being bugged.

Jack and Kat were about to go into high school. Schools nowadays differ from schools of the past. Children went to infant school between the ages of three and six, they went to middle school from the ages of seven to thirteen, and high school started from the age of fourteen to eighteen then they were classed as adults.

Jack and Kat had become quite close over the years; they had formed a powerful bond and spent a lot of time with each other. Jack had to try and forget about Ben as he had been unsuccessful in linking up with him in a dream since the dream he had on the day of the car crash. His mother had done everything she could to try and find out where he was, called in a few favours with some friends she had, but no one had any answers. She was not able to dig too deep for fear of being caught. Anyone found meddling with the affairs of the government usually found themselves being paid a visit by Suits and taken to jail.

Middle school had passed in a blur for the cousins. They mainly spent time studying, away from friends, to not unexpectedly betray their powers or be overheard. Maya had left school not long after Kat and Jack had tested negative. Jack had been particularly vocal in telling everyone that she was responsible for Ben being taken away, that she was a liar and not to be trusted as she could lie about any one of her classmates. Her "mummy" would get them taken away. This caused Maya to leave as everyone turned their back on her for fear of getting reported and disappearing like Ben had. Jack had made it his life's goal to try and find his best friend.

Walking down the road to Kat's house on their first day of high school, he pulled out the photo he had been given by his class teacher all those years ago. It was starting to show some wear and tear now, but it was still the only thing Jack had of him besides his memories to prove he existed. Jack had put it in a small, clear, plastic sleeve to try and preserve the photo. He thought back to his dream, lost in thought for a few moments and had not realised that he had automatically stopped walking just outside Kat's front gate. He sniffed and folded it carefully away just as she came running down the path.

"Morning, Jack," she said with a huge smile, dressed in her new uniform. "Excited for our first day?" Kat was wearing a black blazer with the school crest on it, gold trim around the edges of the sleeves and gold stripes on her tie. She also wore a grey skirt, black tights and a white shirt; her backpack looked brand new. She also had a new haircut, sporting a long bob with layers that framed her thin face nicely. Jack's uniform matched hers, wearing black trousers instead of a skirt, and his black hair was shaved at the sides and long on the top.

"Morning," he replied. "Yeah, I am looking forward to trying for the baseball team. The Smythwater Sealions usually do pretty well in the school league." The two of them walked side by side, chatting about how bad the weather had been over the weekend. A giant dust storm had blown through the town and left a dirty red coating on everything. It had taken Kat's father all weekend to collect as much as he could off the house, the car and the garage to put all over his allotment in the back garden. He stated that the minerals were good for his vegetables and his tomatoes were the best Kat had ever tasted.

The sky had started to turn a dark grey colour and threatened to rain. A slight rumble of thunder could be heard in the distance, so the pair quickened their pace.

Upon arrival at the school, they realised to their surprise that they were not in the same form class. What made things worse was that they appeared to be on opposite sides of the school. They arranged to meet at break time in the lunch hall and headed off to their form rooms to get their attendance mark. Kat was the first to arrive in her room. The teacher looked up from her desk and smiled.

"Hello there, my name is Miss Blakeway. What's yours?" she asked. She was young, slim and pretty, with long, copper coloured hair.

117

"My name is Kathryn Richards, Miss Blakeway. It's nice to meet you," Kat answered politely. She chose a place on the front row, next to the teacher. It was a strategic choice of a seat; Kat wanted to be close to the teacher in case there was any communication that students were unlikely to be informed about, that could be overheard. It also meant that she would not necessarily be spoken to by her classmates, as they would possibly assume that she was a teacher's pet and that she couldn't be trusted. This was completely fine with Kat; she wanted to do her time at school and leave, with as little interaction with the others in her classes as possible.

Kat sat quietly at her desk, looking around the room. The usual government posters were up on the wall in the corner of the room, slogans like "See it, say it!", "Save lives and report Deviants, be your town's hero!" and "Do you really know your neighbour? Trust no one!" jumped out at her. It frightened her to think that one slip up and she would be reported, she tried hard not to think about it much but some worries broke through her wall sometimes, and it kept her awake at night.

Looking out of the window, the rain had started to come down hard, hitting the window like tiny bullets. The clouds were dark, moving fast with the wind and a sudden flash of lightning lit up the sky. Kat loved a good thunderstorm. Things always seemed cleaner after a lot of rain, and colours seemed so much brighter.

The classroom started filling up with new kids from all over the town, she recognised a few from her previous school, and they smiled in acknowledgement

118

when they saw each other, but the majority of them came from another middle school located across town. They were high-fiving each other, pulling each other into hugs and smiling when they arrived. The teacher sat there, watching and observing how they all interacted.

"Right, class," she shouted so she could be heard over the chatter of the group. "My name is Miss Blakeway. It is nice to meet you all. I will now call out names to mark attendance. If you could just raise your hand, say "Here" or "Present", and stand up for a second so everyone can put a face to the name, I would appreciate it. We have an assembly to attend in fifteen minutes, so I would like this done quickly."

She started with Mark Abbotsbury, a young boy covered in freckles, with dirty blonde hair and a cheeky grin. He stood up to cheers from friends from the same middle school and stated his presence. She moved down the list until...

"Ben Phillips?" she said, looking around the room. Kat's stomach did a somersault. *Ben? Here?* The classroom door opened, and a tall, thin lad with blonde hair, blue eyes and glasses stood in the doorway. It was Ben!

"Sorry I'm late, Miss," said Ben." I had to go to the office to find which room I was in."

"Are you Ben Phillips?" asked Miss Blakeway.

"I am, yes, Miss," he replied.

"Then take a seat anywhere, please, Ben. It's lovely to meet you." Ben took a seat at the back of the classroom with empty chairs on either side of him. Miss Blakeway had continued with the attendance, then called out, "Kathryn Phillips?"

119

Kat was still shocked from seeing the friend she thought she had lost years before. She stood up slowly, not taking her eyes off Ben. His eyes locked onto hers from across the room.

"Here, Miss," she answered. She then snapped out of her trance and rushed across to him. He stood up, barely believing his eyes just as Kat threw herself onto him, giving him a hug and crying.

"I thought we would never see you again!" she sobbed onto his shoulder.

"Kat, it's okay. I missed you too," he hugged her tightly.

"Is everything alright here?" their teacher asked. "Kathryn? Are you crying?"

"I'm sorry, I just haven't seen Ben in so long. We were friends when we were six years old and haven't seen each other since," Kat explained. She was now aware that everyone in their class had watched what had happened; many of them seemed confused. The few she went to middle school with looked stunned but those that remembered seemed to understand.

"Please, take a seat," the teacher said. Kat sat down in an empty seat next to Ben, and the teacher continued to take the attendance.

Kat couldn't stop looking at Ben. She dried her tears on her sleeve and looked at him closer. He looked a little gaunt, and his blue eyes seemed to have lost a little of their sparkle. She also noticed that he had scars on the back of his hands too. Knowing some of what he had been through and knowing that she could not utter a single word for fear of being exposed, she was content to just feel thankful that he was alive. Jack had described what he had seen and felt during his dream, and it had given Kat nightmares of her own. She couldn't wait for Jack to see Ben; she couldn't wait to speak to Ben properly herself. Breaktime couldn't come soon enough, but first, they would have to sit through the traditional Genetic Deviation awareness assembly.

Chapter 19 – Reunion

Kat's class joined the rest of her year group in the large sports hall for their first Genetic Deviation assembly of the year. The rain could be heard hammering on the metal roof of the sports hall, Kat hoped it would drown out the sound of whatever was planned for this assembly, but she was sure that the school would ensure that every single word was heard. This assembly was mainly a focus for the school years that were having their tests done that year, but all children had to go to one at least once a year to keep the information fresh in their minds.

Two guards were standing at the front of the hall, dressed the same as the armed guards that Kat and Jack had seen at the test centre. They had not brought along their weapons on this day, however. They stood on either side of a man in a black suit. He stood with his hands behind his back at the front of the hall where everyone could see him, watching the students as they filed into the hall and took their seats on the bleachers.

The hall was almost full when Kat's group turned up. Kat scanned the students' faces around her, trying to find Jack, as she climbed the steps to her form's seats. Kat took her seat, and she leaned to her left to speak to Ben. He was still standing and had turned a ghastly grey colour, sweating and not taking his eyes off the guards standing at the end of the hall.

"Ben," Kat whispered gently, "Are you alright?" She pulled him down into his seat, but he continued to stare at the guards.

The assembly started, and a short video was played for the audience. The main topics were how to spot a deviant, report a deviant, and what to do if someone you love turns out to be a deviant. The students were encouraged to report anything suspicious; just a gut instinct would be enough to open a case for consideration, provided others were willing to put in official statements. However, full-scale investigations would only be launched upon legitimate proof being given.

Ben was having a tough time concentrating. He couldn't tear his eyes away from one of the guards. He recognised him as one of the guards who regularly escorted him to and from places of torture. This man had laughed at him, mocked him and even beat him whilst he was in custody. Ben's mouth had dried up, and he was having difficulty hearing the man in the black suit. The guard was scanning the audience, his eyes scanning across each row of students. His eyes met with Ben's for a split second, Ben felt an uncontrollable, sudden surge in hatred for him. The guard did not seem to recognise him and continued to scan the crowd.

"Sorry, ladies and gentlemen, we seem to be having a problem with the rest of the video," Ben heard the man in the black suit say as his attention came back to the sports hall. "We will try and get it up and running again; bear with us, talk amongst yourselves, please. It is probably because of the weather." The lights had dimmed and flickered and the video had stopped working, but the lights were back up and running immediately. The video was still not working.

"What's going on, Ben?" Kat asked; she looked a little pale herself but was only concerned for her friend's wellbeing.

"It-it's that guard, I-I recognise him," Ben said, his voice was a little shaky, "He w-was there when they were running tests on me." He didn't want to share the unrepeatable details of what happened to him. He still hadn't registered the full horror of what he was subjected to himself and was definitely not prepared to discuss it here, in a room full of people he didn't know or trust.

"It's okay, try not to worry. That man can't do anything to you now, and I am here." She held his hand as she tried to reassure him. She noticed the scars again on his hands and squeezed his hand tightly. He gave her a small squeeze back, and they both continued watching the man in the black suit and his guards trying to fix the video.

After another ten minutes, the school's headmaster called for everyone to be quiet and walked to the front of the hall to speak to the man in the black suit. They seemed to be having a bit of a whispered argument. The man in the suit then moved to the front of the hall once more and started speaking.

"As it looks like we will be unable to continue with our video presentation, I will just talk you through the rest of the assembly and will leave some time for questions at the end," the man in the black suit said as he slowly paced across the width of the hall, all eyes were on him. Kat could feel Ben start to relax a little next to her. He knew he was not suspected of anything and that the assembly would not last forever. He still held on to her hand tightly, appreciative of the support.

"You will all have your second Genetic Deviation test a week after your fourteenth birthdays, which will be during this academic year. Studies have shown that there will be no more tests for you if the second test is negative. If the deviation has not manifested in the first fourteen years of your life, it is not likely to appear at all."

The man in the black suit continued to speak, his voice had a deep authoritarian tone, and nothing but the rain could be heard in the silence when he paused for breath. "The people who test positive, well, they may appear to be harmless, you may have known them all your lives so far, but they cannot be trusted. Deviations can be very dangerous. You may not remember, but almost seven years ago, we discovered a deviant that was the age that you are all now. She killed all four officers that went to her house to take her for more testing."

He stopped pacing and looked around the room, smiling in what he thought was a friendly manner when he looked at the stunned faces in the audience. He opened his arms wide and continued:

"We are the good guys. We look for Deviants for two reasons. The first is that they can be dangerous, as the nature of their deviations can be unpredictable. The second is that they can be useful to us as a population on this planet. If the owner of that deviation is cooperative, that is. This is why it is *crucial* that if there are any amongst you all, we must find out. We are here to help those who need it."

The headmaster then stood up and made his way over to the hall's centre, thanking the guest speaker for his presentation and asking everyone to give him a round of applause. One of the guards went to the side of the room and picked up some leaflets. He gave a pile to the first child in the front row of each of the three sets of bleachers and told them to pass them around. The headmaster continued the assembly, giving out information about breaktimes and lunch procedures.

Jack was sitting on the front row of the bleachers, in the far corner of the audience. He had settled into his form group nicely; he already had some friends from middle school there and had sat with them during the assembly. Jack didn't like the man who was giving the speech; he hated the guards being there too. Taking a leaflet from the pile when it reached him and passing it on, he frowned.

"I wish I was a deviant," his classmate Robin whispered. Robin had sat next to him in his form and knew him previously from his middle school. He was a short, red-haired kid with green eyes. Robin was reading through the leaflet; Jack didn't bother to look at his.

"No, you don't," whispered back Jack. "Don't believe what they say. They don't help Deviants. They wouldn't need the armed guards at the test centre if all they were doing was helping them. We would have heard of them or seen some of them using their abilities too, surely?"

Robin thought about what Jack said and seemed to consider what he was saying.

"You think they are lying?" he asked quietly. He had finished reading the leaflet and scrunched it into a ball. The flyer had reinforced what the man in the black suit had said. It was written in a way that glorified the Deviants, made them appear extraordinary and of great use to the whole of humankind. That they needed to be found, to be helped. Reporting the suspicious behaviour was in everybody's best interests. Reading further, it explained that they could possibly be dangerous if they were not under the government's supervision, as they would not be able to fully explore their Deviations safely. They would then be put to good use for the betterment of everyone.

"I *know* they are lying," Jack replied. "They only help themselves and take advantage of what they can gain from others."

"Being a Deviant may not be such a good idea after all then," Robin said in a small voice. "I think it would be awful to become a slave to the government if you had a power that they found to be useful." He sat back in his seat and sighed, squeezing the paper ball in his hand.

Jack could have elaborated on what he knew and how known deviants were treated after being discovered, but he didn't. It could have led to some awkward questions or even some suspicion directed towards him if any details were too specific. Plus, he was committed to the plan that his family had agreed upon, to not give himself away or compromise their temporary safety. Not when his next test would be in a few weeks' time.

The assembly ended, and everyone from the back row rose from their seats and was dismissed in turn. There was lots of chatter from the students as they made their way towards the exit and their first lesson.

Students started leaving from Kat's row of seats and slowly passed by the row where Jack and Robin were sitting, closest to the exit. Kat and Ben had made their way down the bleachers, as more and more students stood up, they were all trying to leave at the same time which was causing delays. This was causing a crowd to start forming at the exit. Kat had been looking for her cousin when their eyes met as they headed towards the way out.

"Jack! Look!" Kat shouted; her face had completely lit up, and she was smiling her biggest smile. She grabbed Ben's hand and pulled him towards her, pointing at Jack, changing their direction to head towards him.

"No way! Ben?!" Jack's heart flipped in his chest at the sight of the taller, older version of his best friend. He stood up, jumped down from his seat and forced his way through the crowd towards them. He had tears in his eyes. *He was alive! After all this time, he was back!.* The years he had spent worrying about him, mourning his probable death and talking, with hope in his heart, to his photo. Ben turned around and saw Jack pushing his way toward him.

"Jack?" Ben saw his best friend, and a massive rush of emotion surged through his body. "JACK!" he shouted over the noise, pushing toward him. They met in the middle and grabbed each other into a hug.

"I thought you were dead!" Jack said, wiping away tears of happiness. "I missed you so much. I carry

128

your photo with me every day. I never gave up hope." Jack was aware that the lights had flickered out again and heard screams from some girls in the room acting silly.

"Stay calm!" came the headmaster's voice through the semi-darkness. "It's just the weather; I'm on my way to sort it!"

"I couldn't have made it through what I did without you, Jack. For some reason, I knew you were with me, and that kept me going," Ben said. He was still not letting go of his best friend. "I hoped we would meet again. There is so much to tell you..."

"Not here, though. You will have to come over to my house after school. Where do you live now?" asked Jack.

"I live in a small apartment across the town now. It is a lot smaller than our old house, but it is all my dad can afford since he lost his job working with your dad," Ben explained. I will meet you after school, we can walk together. Kat too..." he added as she caught up with them.

They were suddenly aware that they were being watched by a couple of people now, some staff members, some students, as the lights had come back on and most people had already left the hall. They said their goodbyes and headed off to their lessons. All three of them were finally back together and the happiest they had all been in a long time. Jack felt as if he had a weight lifted off his shoulders, his best friend was back, he was alive, and although you could see the haunted look in his eyes, the Ben he knew was still there.

Chapter 20 – Old Friends

Jack had not been in any of Kat or Ben's classes all day. As they all had a disrupted morning with their assembly running longer than expected, their lunch hour was cut short too. All groups in the first year had to eat their lunches in the classroom to make up time. This meant that Jack could not meet up with the others until after school. He could not concentrate on anything his teachers were speaking about in his lessons; he was just so happy that Ben was alive and back with them. He had so many questions to ask him, wondering how he made it out of that awful place. The clock seemed to be slowing down as three o'clock got nearer. He packed up his things, ready to leave as soon as the bell rang. He would not be waiting for his teacher to dismiss him. His only goal was sprinting straight to the gate.

Jack arrived at the gate with minutes to spare. Kat and Ben were walking across the playground towards him. He was smiling so broadly his cheeks were beginning to hurt, but he did not care. They had caught up with him, he grabbed Ben into another hug.

"How are you, Ben?" he asked, looking into his best friend's eyes. He noticed that their bright blue had not changed, but the light in his eyes seemed a little duller.

"It's nice to see you smiling again," Kat said to Jack. "I am guessing Ben has a lot to tell us, so shall we just set off home? We can speak somewhere a little more private, so we are not overheard." She looked pointedly around them as more of their fellow students started filing out of school.

They set off, not really having a destination but just talking, catching up on what had happened at school. All three of them were skating around what had happened to Ben. They spoke about the weather, the events at their middle school and what had happened once Maya had succeeded in getting Ben taken away.

Jack and Kat did not feel safe bringing up Ben's side of what had happened these last six years, as it would mean them admitting that at least one of them had a Genetic Deviance for starters. This was also breaching the agreement that they had with their mothers of not bringing up their powers to anyone. They also knew it was a complex topic for Ben to bring up too, as it looked like he had endured far more than just the one episode of torture that Jack had been a witness to.

Maybe we could tell Ben? Jack thought to himself. He would try and speak to his mom and aunt soon and see if he could be included in their secret. After all, Ben had been treated as a Deviant himself, going through more than anyone else he knew.

They had wandered the streets for over an hour; it was starting to get cold and dark. Kat was getting hungry and said her goodbyes; she left them at the top of her road and ran up her garden path. She was already late home, and her mother would be worried, she waved from her front door, leaving the two of them alone.

"What are you going to do now, Ben? Do you want to come to my house?" asked Jack. He had started to see his breath fogging up the air as the temperature had begun to drop relatively quickly, and neither of them had put on coats. "My mom or dad will give you a lift home from there."

"Sure, that sounds great." Ben smiled. He was happy to be back in the company of people he cared for. He had missed Kat and Ben terribly.

It had been very hard for him and his family since he was released from the test centre. He had been there for about six months, being tested in every way imaginable to try and trigger a response in his genetic makeup. The people torturing him had killed him and brought him back to life more times than he could count. He had been drowned, electrocuted, burned and sliced open. He had been tied to a wheel and spun till he passed out, locked in a room with endless light, locked in a room in complete darkness and even exposed to radioactive elements to try and force a response from his body. He didn't want to relive any of this with anyone, especially Jack or Kat. Ben felt that the look of horror that he would see on their faces would be far worse than having to endure what he had. He may be persuaded to share some of the lesser experiences, but only if he had to.

The pair had finally found themselves on Jack's street, walking slightly faster now the finish line was in sight, the two of them headed for Jack's home. Knocking on the door, Claire answered it with a panicked look on her face but relaxed when she saw her son.

"Oh, thank goodness! I was so worried!" She swept Jack into a hug. "You are so late, young man!" She tried to be firm and strict, but she was just so thankful to have him home in one piece. "And who is…..Ben?

Is that you?" she was shocked to see him, but, knowing how hard her son had been hit with his disappearance, she recovered quickly and hugged him too. "It is so nice to see you again, Ben," she said warmly. She held the door open for them and ushered them inside. "Ben, if you could give me your phone number, I will call your father, so he doesn't worry where you have got to." She grabbed a notepad and a pen from the small table next to the phone and handed it to Ben.

"Hello again, Mrs Roberts," Ben said with a smile. "It's nice to be back." Ben took the pad and paper, scribbling down his number for Claire and passed it back. They made their way into the kitchen, where Jack's mom met them a couple of minutes later and started fixing them plates of sandwiches and a hot drink to ward away the cold.

"Here we go, boys, hot chocolate with marshmallows. It's starting to get pretty chilly out there. Weather reports are saying that we are likely to have an early winter," Jack's mom said. "I'm going to leave you two to warm up, and when you feel ready, Ben, I can take you home, but there is no rush. You are always welcome here."

They chatted and moved straight for the hot chocolate; they didn't realise how cold they were until they had come inside the house. Having tiny moustaches from the drink, they instantly felt warmer, and Ben felt as if no time had passed. He used to love going round to the Roberts' house. Mrs Roberts always had plenty of food to eat and looked after him well when he stayed for sleepovers.

Ben smiled and tucked into the chicken sandwiches left in a large pile on the table. Jack started to eat too, happy that his mom had made Ben feel so welcome and that she had offered to take him home without him having to ask. He stood up, turned on the radio, turned the music up loud and grabbed the wipeable whiteboard from the side of the fridge and a pen. He caught Ben's attention and put his fingers to his lips and pointed to the whiteboard.

Ben looked at him, curious and confused. Jack picked up the pen and started to write:

Do not be alarmed; there are things in this house we do not speak out loud for fear of being overheard... Jack gave Ben a questioning look to see if he had read what had been written, and he nodded. Jack wiped the board clean with his sleeve and started again: *I can't tell you everything yet. I need to talk to the family first. But I was there with you when they were drowning you...*

Ben's eyes widened in shock as he read the whiteboard. He looked up at Jack. He *knew* he wasn't going crazy at the time. He felt his presence with him on that bed, if only for a short while. He held out his hand for the pen, pulled the whiteboard over to himself and used his own sleeve to wipe it clear.

I knew it! You must tell me how! He wrote as small as he could as quickly as he could, wanting to get as much information down in one go. *You saved my life; I almost gave up. It was terrible. I didn't have a positive GD test result. They gave me a test before they let me go. The last 'test' that they did on me was electrocution. They zapped me a couple of times at a very high voltage. It must have been too high; their*

134

machine broke down and caused a power outage. They must have been trying too hard. All I remember is blacking out and waking up in a regular hospital bed.

Jack quickly read what Ben had written and looked up at him. He nodded at Ben, just as his mother walked through the kitchen.

"Wow, that music is a bit loud, isn't it, boys?" she said as she walked over to turn it down. She glanced at the table on the way and saw that they were using the whiteboard. She leaned over Ben to look at it. Ben tried to wipe it clean, but she placed a hand on his arm, stopping him, and continued to read it. He bowed his head, looking at the table. He felt his face flush a deep red and stared at his heavily scarred hands, feeling embarrassed.

After reading the board, Claire was a little shaken, "Oh, Sweetheart. I am so sorry for what you went through." She pulled out a chair and sat next to Ben, and gave him a hug only a mother could. Jack could see that he was crying into his mother's shoulder; his own shoulders were shaking with his sobs. His mother also had a couple of tears running down her face too.

After a few minutes, Ben pulled away. Jack saw that he had managed to calm himself, so he got up and turned off the music.

"Would anyone like a cup of tea?" he asked. He switched the kettle on and set some cups on the table. A cup of tea was his family's go-to solution to make anyone who was upset, feel better. If anyone needed a cup right now, they did.

Jack noticed that his mom had cleared the whiteboard and was writing on it herself. Her small,

135

neat handwriting meant that she could write a great deal on there without having to keep wiping it clean. She had had a lot of practice on it over the years; she wrote one message to the boys before getting up to finish the tea for Jack:

We will sort this out, both of you, try not to worry. We will make sure that the government cannot do this again. It will take time and planning, but I think that you two may be able to help. We need to go for a drive to speak openly. Ben, we will give you more information very soon, but you must not tell anyone. Okay? Our lives depend on us being able to keep this secret.

Claire laid out the tea and looked questioningly at Ben, checking that he had read and understood her message. He still had tears in his eyes, but he nodded, feeling more optimistic after sharing something so terrible. He had not even been able to speak to his parents about what had happened. Jack wiped the board clean and replaced it.

"Here we go, a lovely cup of tea," Jack's mom said. "I can take you home then if you like, Ben?"

"Yes, please, Mrs Roberts, I have missed coming here." Ben didn't want to go home, he now lived in a rougher part of town, and his apartment was a lot smaller than the house they used to live in. It was cold, and having the heater on used too much electricity. The electricity that they could not afford to waste, as it was expensive, and Jack's father was now working as an office clerk and was not making half of what he used to when he was working with Jack's dad.

The car journey took about half an hour to get to Ben's home. The weather had taken a bit of a turn and it had started to rain quite hard. Eventually, they all pulled up outside a rundown block of apartments on a darkened street in the middle of town. The streetlight outside the entrance to the building was not working, which made the place look even more foreboding. The rain had finally stopped again.

"Well, here we are. Thank you for the ride, Mrs Roberts."

"Please, call me Claire, Ben." Jack's mom said with a smile. "See you soon, Honey."

Ben got out of the car as his father appeared at the block's front door. He smiled and waved at Jack and his mom and started down the stairs to have a talk with them.

Michael Phillips was a tall man with blonde hair, like his son. He also had blue eyes and the posture of someone who has spent a lot of time in the armed forces. Having worked with Jack's father for a long time, at one point he knew Claire and Jack well. However, since Ben got taken away all those years ago, he had lost touch with the Roberts family.

"Hiya Claire, Jack. How are you both doing?" he asked. He shivered slightly; he hadn't anticipated the cold when he left his apartment. "Thank you, Claire, for bringing Ben home. Janice and I appreciate it."

"It wasn't any bother, Mick. We are both doing well. How are things with you and Jan?" Claire asked. She used to go drinking with his wife many years ago. Before they both got pregnant anyway.

"She's at work now. I will tell her you asked after her, though, it has been a little tough with us both having to juggle work and make sure someone is at home for Ben when he gets home, but we are

137

managing. Hoping to get some form of a job back with the government soon, I may not get my old position back, but maybe I can be of some use to someone." You could tell he was doing his very best to sound upbeat, especially as Ben was standing right next to him, but there was a slight crack in his voice as he spoke that betrayed how he was truly feeling.

"Well, if you ever fancy coming over for dinner, you are more than welcome. Just let us know what day is best for you. Maybe we can break out some board games and make a whole evening out of it." Claire suggested. "But you both should get in out of the cold, it is starting to rain again, and we don't want you getting ill."

"That's true, come on, Ben," Mick said, putting an arm around his son. "Let's get inside. Thanks again, Claire. We shall see you soon."

"Bye, Claire. See you tomorrow, Jack." Ben said. Ben felt so happy saying those words. He never thought he would hear himself repeating them out loud again.

"Bye!" The Roberts' said, together. "See you tomorrow, Ben!" shouted Jack.

Claire started the car again, and the two of them headed home. Neither one of them spoke, both lost in their thoughts. They were headed back to an empty house as Captain Roberts was away for the next few days on a business trip.

When they arrived home, Jack decided to go straight to bed. He had been through a lot today, feeling well and truly drained. Jack was happy, though, having his best friend back. He took Ben's photo out of his pocket and put it in the corner of his notice board on his bedroom wall, feeling confident that there was no need to carry it around with him every day, now that he had him around in person. However, he would still keep the photo to remind him of what he thought he had lost.

Jack lay in bed thinking about the afternoon's events. He felt an overwhelming admiration for his best friend, the pain and horror he had gone through, yet he still managed to smile and carry on the way he did. Jack didn't think that forgiveness would come easy if the circumstances were reversed. He felt that he would be looking for vengeance on the people that had hurt him. Revenge on *everyone* concerned, including Maya. He would make sure he killed her for starting the whole thing off. Maybe he would do that anyway if their paths ever crossed again... He didn't think he would be able to control himself for what she had done to Ben. If Ben didn't kill her, he would make sure he did instead, or die trying.

Chapter 21 – Old Dreams Die Hard

Jack was being driven in a luxurious, leather seated car, moving towards the large, white building with a high, black-metallic fence surrounding it again. He was alone this time, sitting in the back of the car with tinted windows and was wearing a very well made black suit. The car slowed as it came to the large metal gates at a checkpoint. Jack lowered the window, and a young man in a uniform welcomed him, ticking his name off a list he had on a clipboard. The gates were then opened by another man in a smart uniform. Two armed guards were standing at either side of the gate, all dressed in black. They could hardly be seen in the light on this cloudy evening. The car pulled up to the building entrance, and Jack got out of the vehicle. Jack realised that he was not in his own body again from the height he was looking from and knew he had entered one of his real-time dreams.

He headed towards the building, noting how many armed guards were stationed along the walk. As he passed, each one jumped to attention and saluted him.

"Good evening, Sir," some of them had said before standing in their previous position and staring straight ahead once more. More people stopped, saluted him, or nodded their heads in his direction as he entered the building. The body of the man he was in, Jack guessed, was a powerful man; he could feel the man's emotions and felt indestructible.

Jack was shown to his seat by a very slim, pretty woman. He followed her to a VIP box. A waiter inside was standing to attention, waiting to take his drink order, and the six seats there were soft, squashy, and very comfortable. He glanced out of the box and saw the stage from his previous dream on his left. It had a bright red floor, a faded hilly landscape painted on the back wall and lots of lights on the ceiling. Some of the paint looked as if it were peeling from the landscape, showing its age. To his right, the seating looked like that of a stadium. It was staggered into five layers that held hundreds of people, forming a semi-circle around the stage. People were standing in the middle of the semi-circle, down below. He noticed that they were not following the apparent dress code; some looked a little unkempt.

A waiter appeared by his side with a drink. Jack's hand reached up and took it, placing it on a small table next to his reclining chair. The lights dimmed, as they had done the last time Jack was here. A spotlight appeared in the middle of the stage, which expanded to fill the whole of it. He reached for his drink and settled into his seat to enjoy the show. Jack turned his attention to the stage as the happy, bouncy music began, and a group of people appeared from a secret entrance on the floor of the middle of the stage. They were all lined up in a row with huge smiles on their faces and began to dance.

This whole performance was different from the last time he saw it; Jack noticed many more children in this show. To his horror, he saw something that he had not detected through the eyes of his six-year-old self. Something had seemed strange about those people, the way they had moved seemed off all those years ago, but all that could be remembered was that

141

they looked happy as they all had huge smiles on their faces. This time, however, he saw why. They had metal hooks that looked like they were looped around the back of their heads, hooked into the corners of their mouths, holding them open into a smile. He also noted long, clear bars strapped to the wrists and ankles of the performers, which is why they seemed so rigid in their movements. Their eyes were open wide in fear, searching the crowd for help that would not come. The music stopped, and the dancers moved closer to the front of the stage. They all leaned forward and took a bow, but no one clapped. He heard a faint, metallic whirring, and then a wire moved very quickly from above the stage to the bottom, and the heads of the dancers fell to the floor, thumping as they landed. Their bodies slumped forward on their knees, draining into the thin metal grate that had been hardly visible on the floor of the stage.

Blood also sprayed into the silent, standing room audience, and he realised, with revulsion, that they were dressed in the same outfits as the dancers on the stage. Every single one of them had their mouths pulled back into horrifying smiles, and they were all chained together. There had to be at least a hundred of them.

Jack screamed, as loud as his lungs would allow. He heard the scream come from the lungs of the man whose eyes he was unwillingly witnessing these horrors through. Most of the audience turned and looked towards his box.

"Are you alright, Sir?" the waiter asked.

"I am fine, young man. I don't know what happened." Jack's stomach dropped, and his heart

almost stopped beating in fright. He recognised that voice. Suddenly he knew whose body he was in. It was that of his father.

"AAAAHHHH!" Jack shouted, clapping his hand to his head. He knew this pain was temporary, but this was the worst it had felt coming out of a dream. Sweaty and shaking, he rolled over onto his side and threw up over the side of his bed. His mother was not in his room like she usually was. Staggering to his feet, almost blind with the pain in his head, he hastily made his way by touch to her bedroom.

"Mom? Where are you?" he asked. His vision had started to clear, and the agonising pain he had felt had now diminished to a dull ache.

"I am downstairs, Honey. Is everything alright?" she appeared at the bottom of the stairs with a cup of tea in one hand, mobile phone in the other. She had been chatting to her sister and not heard him shout.

Jack made his way downstairs, passed his mother and made straight for the whiteboard in the kitchen. He quickly scribbled four words onto it and grabbed his coat. *WE NEED TO TALK.* She took one look at him and cancelled the call without another word to Liz.

Claire picked up her coat and car keys, glancing at the clock. It was quarter to twelve. For the sake of anyone who may have been listening, she said out loud: "Fancy a midnight snack? Let's go for ice cream."

"Yes, please, Mom. That would be amazing." Jack answered out loud, again for the sake of appearances. His headache had almost passed, but his heart was still hammering hard inside his chest. His father? What

143

was he doing there? Was that even real? He had a hundred questions whizzing around in his head, and he needed to tell his mom. There was a possibility that they could be in very real danger. His father appeared to be entirely different from the man he thought he was.

Like most car journeys they shared, the car journey to the ice cream parlour was silent. Jack's mom had managed to conceal her own gift by being extra careful and vigilant. Even if their car and house had not been bugged, she was still not prepared to take that risk. They pulled up for ice cream, just in case the vehicle had a tracker on it, and both ordered a chocolate and peanut butter scoop each. They had found this place once by accident, but as it was open till 3am every night and had a field with some benches on it, it was the perfect place to go to not be overheard if they were cautious.

Jack and Claire made their way to the farthest bench at the end of the field. The rain had eased for a little while, and although it was still cloudy, the bench itself was dry as it was covered by a giant umbrella.

"Right, tell me everything," his mother said, looking straight at him from across the bench. "Leave nothing out. What has happened?"

Jack launched into what he saw, his mother said she vaguely remembered him telling her about a dream in that building before, but she could not remember the details as clearly as Jack could. When he got to the part where the dancers bowed and their demise, she gasped, her hand covering her mouth and eyes open wide in shock. She looked terrified when he

144

mentioned that he saw all of it through his father's eyes.

"We are in much more trouble than I thought." She said to her son in a low voice. "You must understand that I know as much as you do about your father's line of work. He is bound by his contract to not speak about what he does. As much as I love him, I know we have done the right thing, not telling him about us. We need to put together a plan to get away from here. I have some friends who could help. They are part of an underground resistance...."

"Mom, we need to tell Kat and Aunty Liz. We need to tell Ben too. He may start asking around if we don't give him a decent explanation of how I knew what was happening when he was being tortured. If he says the wrong thing in front of Dad..." his voice trailed into silence. They both sat there for a while. Their ice cream sat on the bench, untouched and melting slowly. Claire had her head in her hands with her eyes shut. A single tear ran down her left cheek.

"Right, I have an idea, it should work, but it will take time; we need to get you and Kat through your GD tests again first. If we disappear before then, it will cause people to start looking for us." Claire said. Her mind was whirring away. She needed time to think over what she had just heard. She had not foreseen this happening in any of her premonitions, which worried her greatly. She would go back and start searching with her mind and forecast what the current future held in store for them. "We need to act no different towards your father when he gets home, or he could become suspicious. I need to speak to some people and you need to tell Ben everything. Kat needs to know what happened tonight, I will tell your aunt. I'll go to see her tomorrow morning." Claire stood up, picked up her ice cream and threw it in the bin. Jack did the same, and they headed home.

Chapter 22 – The Truth Will Out

Jack had managed to get a little sleep after the events of the night before, but he was still exhausted. He had woken up earlier than he usually would for a school day but wanted to speak to his mom before school if he could. He got ready and made his way into the kitchen, where he found her, sat at the kitchen table. His mother looked like she hadn't been to sleep at all. She was still dressed in the clothes she wore last night; her ponytail had started to fall out too. She was staring at the window, but the curtains were still closed, it was raining hard, it could be heard hitting the glass. The radio had been turned on and played the chart-toppers of the last five years. A cold cup of coffee was untouched next to her on the table.

"Morning, Mom," Jack said as he helped himself to a glass of orange juice and a bowl of cereal. When she didn't reply, he looked up at her. Her eyes had clouded over and had a swirling fog where her irises were meant to be. He was a little startled. He had never seen his mom use her power before. He noticed the whiteboard on the table next to her had some writing on it:

If I am still in a vision when you come in, just place your hand on my shoulder. I will come back. Love you, Mom XXX

He stood at his mother's side and gently placed his hand on her shoulder. She took a deep breath as if she had been startled, and her eyes suddenly returned to normal. She saw him and smiled.

"Morning, Honey," she said. "How are you doing today?" She wiped the whiteboard clean and returned it to the fridge, keeping it in place with magnets. She then put her coffee in the microwave to heat it back up and turned off the radio.

"I'm okay, thanks. I just wondered what the plan for today was," Jack said, with a pointed look at her.

The microwave pinged. Claire took her coffee out of the microwave, gave it stir and sipped at it, returning to her seat. She paused for a moment and then spoke:

"I think we ought to go round to see your aunt after school. If Ben comes back with you for tea, we can maybe get pizza, and all eat together?"

"Sounds good. Any chance I can phone Ben whilst he is still at home so he can ask his folks?" he asked in-between mouthfuls of choco-hoops.

"Sure, go ahead," Claire said, "I'm just going upstairs to get changed. I can meet you in the car in ten minutes." Her visions had given her a lot to think about. She could control what or who she saw, but because of it being the future and the fact that nothing is set in stone, she could not entirely rely on what she had seen to be completely accurate. If she did anything to intervene, she would have to look again to see what had changed if she did anything to intervene, or she could be unpleasantly surprised.

She had seen her husband in a fury like no other. He was a completely different man from the one she had married. She was a little confused as to what had made him so angry but she knew it wasn't too far into the future. She had also seen Kat, Jack and Ben and knew that they were also in danger, running through a

148

field that had tall crops growing in it as if their lives depended on it. She decided that she needed more information before she decided to intervene. This is how she remained hidden. She was cautious and did not take risks. She only tried to change the future to keep her family safe, and so far, she had been successful, but she knew it was only a matter of time before her luck ran out or she irreversibly changed the future with no positive outcome. Only time would tell. She needed to contact her old friend Kyle; he would do what he could to help her or at least he would know someone who would.

Later that day, Claire had parked her car and waited outside the school for Kat, Jack and Ben to finish so they could all go over to Liz's house. She had come up with the skeleton of a plan to get them all into hiding. They needed to use her sister's power. She could communicate to people without speaking aloud; Claire just hoped her sister could get her brother-in-law out of the house this evening.

The kids all came out of school simultaneously; they piled into the back of the car, and they headed over to Kat's house. It didn't take Liz long to convince her husband, John, to go out and watch the football and have some drinks at a bar with his friends, leaving them in peace to tell Ben what had gone on and to try and come up with a plan of escape.

They arrived at Kat's house, and were greeted at the door by her mother. They all made their way into the kitchen, taking seats and chatting loudly.

"Where is it? I know it is here somewhere," Kat's mom said, her head under the sink, looking for something. She stood up, opened a cupboard and began searching through it. Claire quickly ran around her sister's house and made sure the doors into the house were locked, and the curtains closed in every room.

"When are you going to tell me what is going on then?" Ben said to Jack and Kat. The pair of them, eyes wide, put their fingers to their lips and were signalling to be quiet. "What's wrong with you two?" he continued. He was a little confused as to why everyone seemed to be acting strangely all of a sudden.

"Ah! Here it is!" Liz said, holding an old, battery-powered radio in the air triumphantly. She put it on, louder than she usually would have and then took Ben's wrist quickly. He looked at her, wondering why she had grabbed him when he heard her voice inside her head:

Don't panic, it's me, Liz. I am a Deviant. There is no easy way to tell you this but we all are.

He pulled his arm away, looking scared and stood up.

"Come on, Ben, you *know* us. We will not harm you," Liz said to him. She held out her hands again, and he slowly put his hands in hers.

We have all decided to be completely honest with you about our situation, as we trust you. You can choose to carry on, as usual, telling no one about us, and we will do our best to protect you if, and when, the time comes. Or, you can choose to turn us over to the government and reap the rewards, which I imagine would be pretty substantial for handing over four deviants, knowing what you will be subjecting us to if you did. So, can we trust you?

150

Ben turned pale. He looked around the room; the other three looked at him with serious faces. Ben cared for these people and considered them part of his family in his heart of hearts. He nodded at Liz. The others relaxed their stares, Jack pulled a pizza menu towards him and started chatting to Claire about toppings.

"We felt that we owed you an explanation as to how we came to know of your treatment, whilst you had been taken away for testing. We use the radio to distract anyone who may have bugged our homes when speaking about, or using our powers. It all started with Jack. Jack has a deviation that allows him to see people and what they are doing whilst he is asleep. He saw you and witnessed you being tortured in a water tank. Jack was also there when you were murdered and brought back. He said you could feel his presence at some point? He said he felt you acknowledge him and mentioned his name under your breath? You can think of your reply. I will hear it. It will be as if you were talking to me." Liz explained in as much detail as she could.

"Yes, I could sense that he was in the room with me. I didn't know that he was watching or feeling any of it, though," Ben thought back, feeling a little awkward that his best friend has seen a little part of what he desperately tried to forget.

"Claire and I managed to pull some strings with some people we know, to try and get you released. I cannot give you any more information than that, for the safety of the people who help us. Do you understand?" Ben nodded once more. Liz let go of

Ben's hand and gave him some time to process his thoughts.

Things were slowly making a little more sense to him, but the shock of them all being deviants without being detected? That was unheard of. He looked across at Kat and Jack, who seemed to be arguing whether pineapple on a pizza was allowed. He could not hear anything other than Liz's voice when she spoke to him, but whilst she allowed him time to let the new information sink in, the noise returned from the rest of the room.

Liz then took his hand in hers again and began to fill him in on the rest of the group's powers. That Kat could heal herself, Claire had premonitions and could see the future. Liz could read minds herself, communicate telepathically when touching that person, and manipulate people's emotions. Jack had dreams, most of them in real-time, some in other times, and could see through the eyes of the people in those dreams. Ben's mind was spinning, but he understood everything and would not break their trust. Ben felt honoured that they were willing to tell him such a secret as they all knew what would happen if they were discovered and reported. What puzzled him most was how Jack and Kat had both passed their first test almost seven years ago, but he knew better than to ask.

"Right, I think we have had enough bickering about pineapple. Shall I order pizzas now?" asked Claire. "I'm starving. Ben, what toppings would you like?"

"I think I will go with a pepperoni, please," he said with a grin, "but no pineapple." Kat and Jack laughed as Claire called the pizza place with their order. When she returned, they turned the radio up a little louder. Claire pulled her whiteboard out of a backpack she brought along with her. She pulled the pen lid off with her teeth and began to write: *Liz will try and speak to us all simultaneously. In theory, we should all hear each other but please, no side conversations. She has never done this before, so please be patient.*

Everyone read the board and nodded, Claire wiped the board clean whilst Liz rolled up her sleeves. She needed everyone to be touching her to communicate with them, so everyone needed to be holding on together. She lay her bare arms flat in front of her on the table, closed her eyes, and everyone gently placed a hand on them. After a minute, only the radio could be heard.

Liz had never stretched her powers this far before. She wasn't entirely convinced it would work when Claire suggested she try it. Claire had popped round earlier that day to discuss Jack's most recent dream and to try and figure a way to get them all to safety. They had one or two friends that they could trust between them to help them disappear. That privilege came with knowing people who worked for the government. However, only the people in that room and one other knew of Liz and Claire's abilities, and, the way she saw it, they inevitably would end up using them to barter their freedom.

As each group member slowly put their hands on her forearms, she immediately accessed their thoughts. She felt worry coming from Claire and confusion from Ben. Kat's main thought was about the pizza winging its way over to them shortly. Jack was dwelling upon what he had seen through his father's eyes and had somehow managed to put up a bit of a wall to stop her from looking too far. She wouldn't have needed long to break his defences, but other matters were far more pressing. She made a mental note to speak to him and Claire about it separately as she may be able to help him develop his powers to more than just the occasional dream.

"Can everyone hear me in their minds?" Liz sent to the others, opening her eyes for a few moments. They all nodded. *"It worked!"* She closed her eyes once more but smiled. She had not pushed her powers like this before. She surprised herself with how she was managing to communicate with more than one person at a time. *"Okay, Claire and I have come up with a shell of a plan to keep you, Kat and Jack, from getting positive GD results. What we did last time may be too risky to do again, so we are enlisting the help of a friend this time, so do not worry. Claire has foreseen this working. Also, we now need to develop a plan to get out of Smythwater for good. We now also know that Martin is a dangerous man and definitely cannot be trusted."*

Liz felt Kat and Ben's emotions shift slightly to confusion, questioning why. Jack's emotions were, again, closely guarded and hard to read. She opened her eyes for a second and saw that Jack's face was utterly blank. She wondered what he was doing to block her and whether or not he was doing it on purpose. Closing her eyes again, she launched into a quick explanation, more for Kat and Ben's benefit, as to what Jack had seen. She then told them that they would find a way to get them out, but only after they had passed their tests. Maybe they could go and visit Grandma?

"Liz?" a small voice interjected. *"Can I ask something?"* It was Ben. He had been nothing but polite and quiet for the entire time she had known him. Even after what had happened to him, she was impressed and shocked by how well he had handled himself.

"Go ahead, Ben. We are all listening." Liz replied.

"When you guys leave, can I come with you? Please? I don't think I could handle losing you all again, and maybe my Mom and Dad could come too?" Ben asked. The raw emotion Liz could feel as he asked the group caused a tear to run down Liz's cheek. It was becoming too much for her to keep the conversation together with so many people inside her head. The longer they stayed there, the more of their feelings she felt.

"We will do our very best to incorporate you into our plan, Ben if that is how you feel." This time it was Claire who answered. She was aware that their time was running short, the pizza would be there any moment, and she doubted that Liz would be able to hold the conversation for much longer, with it being her first time attempting this. *"Maybe we should all leave Liz to her own thoughts now and get ready for some food?"*

As Claire opened her eyes, she saw that the kitchen was in darkness. She assumed that there had been a power cut and went outside to the fuse box, where she saw the neighbour outside doing the same thing and waved. The others continued to listen to the radio and lit some candles, putting them around the middle of

155

the table. Claire tripped the fuse box a couple of times before she saw the neighbour's house light back up again. She tried once more, and the garden lit up with the light from her sister's house, just in time for the pizza delivery man to walk up the path with their order.

They passed the rest of the night playing cards and enjoying each other's company. Liz and Claire shared a look across the table as they were playing. They would have to enjoy these nights whilst they could. Things looked like they were about to get very complicated and very messy.

Chapter 23 – Complications

Claire and Liz had told the kids that they were to draw no attention to themselves and focus on their schoolwork. Kat would have her GD test first, and they needed to arrange it so she would pass her test. The three of them did their very best to keep out of trouble. Ben would end up at Jack's house after school, staying over most weekends, and Claire dropped him back home whenever he needed to be back.

On the other hand, Kat had an after-school club that she attended twice a week for an extra mathematics qualification. She stayed behind on Wednesdays and Fridays until four thirty with a group of about fifteen other kids in her year. During Friday's lesson, the group was given a task for the following week. Kat had to teach the class about Pythagoras' Theorem, with examples and questions for the group. She wanted to ask the teacher how best to give the presentation at the end of the lesson, so she stayed behind. The rest of the class filed out quickly, leaving her alone with the teacher. She took notes on the advice given by the teacher and gathered her things. Her mother would be waiting for her near the school gates in the car as usual.

As she left the classroom, making her way down the corridor towards the playground, she realised she was being followed by a burly older girl who looked in one of the years above her. She quickened her pace but it was matched by her follower. She pulled open the door at the end of the corridor and stepped onto the playground.

"Hey! You!" the girl shouted to Kat. "Stop where you are!"

Kat ignored the girl and continued to walk quickly towards where her mother waited for her. The school entrance was on the other side of the playground, and she would then be in sight of her mom. She didn't have far to go...

"I said, stop!" the girl shouted. She was panting slightly; Kat could have easily outrun her but did not want to appear frightened. She was pretty happy to stop but knew a hostile encounter with this girl would not end well.

Kat was almost running now; she had made it through the gates, the girl was very close to catching her up. She saw her mom's car, she waved her arms, her mom flashed the car lights to show she had seen her and started the engine. The girl grabbed Kat's arm and spun Kat around.

"Hey! Get your hands off me!" Kat said with a snarl. She grabbed the girl's hand and pulled it off her arm.

"You have no idea who I am, but I know who you are, Kathryn." The girl said in a low voice. "I am Stacey; Maya is my cousin, and you *will* pay for what you did to her." Stacey was a whole head taller than Kat and very thick-set. She had eyes that were almost black in colour, her black hair blew across her acne-covered face and she was also wearing braces. Her size alone earned her enough respect around the school that ensured she was not bullied.

"I don't care who you are. You want to tell Maya to come and threaten me herself and not send someone else to do it for her," Kat said coolly. "And Maya will be the one who will pay if we ever see *her* again. I will make sure of that myself."

She turned around and started walking again to the car. Liz had got out and stood next to the car, looking over at the encounter her daughter was having.

"Don't worry, I *will* catch up with you very soon!" Stacey shouted as Kat crossed the road. "You can be certain of that, Kathryn!"

"Who was that?" Liz asked Kat as they both got back into the car.

"Apparently, that is Maya's cousin, and she is going to make me pay for what we did to her...." Kat told her mother. She was a little shocked that someone would threaten her for something they did as children almost seven years ago.

"You must be careful, Kat", her mother warned. "Do not forget what they managed to do with Ben. That family have a few useful contacts within the government that we would not like to get mixed up with, remember?"

"I remember, don't worry." Kat mumbled, she was staring out of the window as the car moved. She wondered where Maya had been all this time. She had left their middle school not long after Kat and Jack had gotten their results back from their GD tests. No one had seen or heard from her; rumour had it, the whole family had left town.

"At least it is the weekend now, eh?" her mom said, trying to sound more positive. "You have anything exciting planned?"

159

"No, I have a lot of schoolwork to do, so I am just going to stay in and see how much I can get done," she replied. "Besides, Jack and Ben are going to the cinema with Uncle Martin and Aunty Claire; Ben is sleeping over there this weekend."

They arrived home, and Kat decided to start her assignment when she got in. She did not let Stacey or her empty threats cross her mind again. Kat really did not care what others thought of her; the only thing she was bothered about was keeping up appearances with everyone at school and her impending GD test coming up in four weeks. She turned on some music and settled down to an evening of work.

The following couple of weeks passed by in a blur. Kat had received top marks for her presentation and continued to work really hard at school. Ben and Jack had also been busy. Jack had signed up for the Baseball team and was at practice every Monday, Wednesday and Friday, out on the school fields. Ben liked to stay and watch the practice; he would still go home with Jack and have dinner with Jack and his family.

Kat had stayed behind again one Wednesday for her extra mathematics lesson. She decided to walk over to the school fields to catch up with Ben and Jack. Jack's practice ran over half an hour later than her lesson did, so she had enough time to meet them.

She packed up her equipment and said goodbye to her teacher. She headed towards the building's exit and heard footsteps behind her. It was Stacey again.

"Well, well, well..." she began, "Look who it is."

"Whatever, Stacey, just leave me alone," Kat said, trying to push the door open. It was heavy and hard to push it open when a sign said: *PULL*.

"I don't think I will," said Stacey, moving closer to Kat. She had a horrible smirk on her face that twisted her features and accentuated the deep scars her acne had left. She looked very menacing in the afternoon light.

Kat had finally worked out why the door was not opening and wrenched it open. Stacey pushed it closed again and smacked Kat's head against the door. She saw stars for a second but shook them off. She shoved Stacey back and tried again with the door. Again, Stacey blocked her from leaving. She grabbed Kat by the hair and headbutted her nose. It instantly broke, and blood splattered everywhere.

Kat had reached a boiling point, and, given the fact that she could feel her nose healing already, she grabbed Stacey by the throat and twisted the sinews and vocal cords as far around as she could. Stacey fell to her knees, clutching at her throat, choking and weakly trying to pull Kat's hand away. Kat then brought her own knee up to Stacey's face, feeling pretty sure that if she hadn't broken her nose in return, she would have at least given her two black eyes. She then crouched down next to the bully, who was now lying on the floor covering her face and whimpering. She whispered:

"Let's forget this ever happened because there is plenty more where that came from. I suggest you leave me and my family alone. Tell Maya I said hello."

She stepped over Stacey, leaving her nose bleeding, still choking and spluttering on the ground and continued to the fields towards Jack and Ben, who were just leaving the pitch and heading towards the changing rooms.

"Hey Kat, wow! What happened to you?" asked Ben. "Are you alright? There's blood on your shirt!"

"I'm fine. I am not hurt." She said, looking around.

"Here, take my shirt," Jack said, passing Kat his shirt out of his bag. "I'll keep my t-shirt on from practice, and no one will see to ask you questions then."

"Thanks, Jack," Kat said. She gratefully accepted Jack's shirt and jumped into the girls changing rooms to change her shirt and hide the blood. She caught her reflection in the mirror and spotted a red streak on her face where blood had smeared. Washing it off and tidying herself up, Kat hid her stained shirt in her own bag and went back outside to meet the others to walk home.

During the walk home, she told the boys all about Stacey and what happened, how she had threatened Kat a few weeks beforehand and what she had done that afternoon. They were shocked that she was still willing to try and attack Kat on Maya's behalf after all the time that had passed, and even more shocked at what Kat had done in retaliation.

Chapter 24 – Consequences

The following day, Kat woke up early with a horrible feeling in the pit of her stomach. She hoped that the scuffle she had with Stacey the day before was kept quiet, but she very much doubted it. Jack and Ben both agreed that none of them should be at school alone after usual hours, so Kat decided to go straight to Jack's baseball practice after her lesson was over and meet Ben and her cousin there.

She dressed and made her way downstairs; her mother was sitting at the table in the kitchen drinking a cup of coffee.

"Morning." Her mom said, as Kat sat down opposite her and started pouring herself some cereal. "You do know that there is inevitability going to be some fallout from yesterday, don't you?"

"What do you mean?" Kat asked. "I am fine. There's no proof she hurt me." She started munching on her cereal. Kat had told her mother everything as soon as she got home, she had shown her the blood stained shirt and even admitted to what she did to Stacey.

"But *you* hurt *her*." Her mom replied. "You may have come out of it unharmed," she continued, looking wearily around the room and choosing her words carefully, "But from the sound of it, *she* didn't. She will have had to explain her injuries somehow. You are not injured at all. It comes across as a little suspicious…" Liz's face had suddenly lit up. "Hang

163

on, I have had an idea. I need to make a quick phone call. You will be a little late for school."

Kat was left alone at the table, a little confused as to what her mother was thinking but continued to eat her cereal. Her mother had dashed off upstairs after making a quick call and came down a couple of minutes later with an armful of her makeup.

"Right, we are going to put some of this on for the next couple of days. You need to make sure people know it is hurting and act like you are in a bit of pain with it. You must follow this through, Kat or people could become suspicious."

"I understand, Mom," Kat answered. She sat quietly whilst her mother applied the makeup to her face mixing a hue of blue and purple eyeshadows, blending them around one of Kat's eyes and on her nose. Not too much, as they would have to use it for a week or two to keep up appearances. The colouring of the bruising would change, but initially, the bruising would be dark blue and purple in colour.

"There we go, sweetheart, all done," Liz smiled, admiring her handiwork. She took a photo of her daughter's face on her phone, so she knew what the bruise would need to look like the next morning when they repeated the exercise. "Finish getting ready for school, and I will drop you off. Remember, it hurts, but it is not broken."

Kat made it to school an hour late in the end, but as her mom had done an outstanding job with the make-up, everyone forgave her tardiness. However, Jack gave her a questioning look across the table at lunch. She shook her head in reply, and he shrugged, continuing to eat his sandwich and listened to Ben

164

talking about a computer game he had borrowed from his cousin.

"She is over there! I broke her nose, I heard it snap and there was blood everywhere, her nose was all smashed up, then it had suddenly stopped bleeding!" came a hoarse, voice from across the room. The lunch hall volume dropped instantly; many people looked around for the voice owner. It was Stacey; she was trying to shout at one of the lunchtime supervisors and pointing towards Kat. She had some very dark bruising around her throat, and her nose was pretty swollen. Kat felt a little bad for her; she must have done some damage to her throat from the sound of her voice.

Eventually, the inevitable happened; a teacher Kat did not know came up to their table.

"Are you Kathryn Richards?" the teacher asked. He was young, very tall, had glasses and a patchy beard.

"Yes, Sir. I am." Kathryn replied. She instantly liked this teacher, he seemed friendly, and he smiled at her.

"Great. If you could gather your things and follow me, please. I have to take you to see the headteacher." Kathryn felt a little worried, but she knew that they would not send a new teacher to come and escort her if it had been too serious. It would have been a senior member of staff that she knew.

"Catch you later, guys," Kat said to Jack and Ben. "Meet me at the gates after school if I don't see you beforehand."

Both of her unconcerned companions said goodbye and continued to chat with each other. If they did anything other than that it could cause them to look suspicious and they could be in big trouble. Both of them glanced at each other nervously as they continued with their conversation. Kat picked up her things and left.

She followed the new teacher down the corridors towards the headmaster's office. She stayed behind him for the entire journey, racking her brains as to why she may have been summoned. It had to be the fight with Stacey, surely?

They walked quickly. This new teacher seemed a little unsure of where he was headed. He weaved around the students heading towards the canteen and ascended the stairs instead of descending them.

"Excuse me, Sir?" Kat said, feeling a little confused but still following him. "We are going the wrong way. We need to go downstairs…." Her feeling of instantly liking this teacher was ebbing away fast. The further away they walked from the headteacher's office, the worse she began to feel.

"This way, Miss Richards, please, the headmaster is not in his office." He spoke loudly and continued his pace along the next corridor, this one clear of all people. He stopped suddenly outside a classroom, peered through the glass pane and tried the door. The classroom was in darkness, and the door was locked. He looked around and pulled out his keys, looking for the correct one for that block. With a resounding *click*, the door was open. He pushed the door, indicating that Kat should step inside.

"Sir, what's going on?" Kat did not trust this man at all now. He glanced around the room and gestured for her to take a seat. She did not take a seat but slowly walked into the darkened room and made

166

towards the light switch. The teacher stayed by the door, glancing through the glass pane again to ensure they were not interrupted.

"Leave the lights off, please, Kathryn. What I have to say will not take long." The teacher was sweating now and seemed a little twitchy, almost like he was holding something back or excited about something. "I know you are a Deviant. I have been watching you for some time now. You don't know me because I am supposed to not be seen by potential targets, until it is too late."

Kat gasped. Her time had run out.

"Potential targets?" Kat asked, "What does that mean? Who are you? What do you want?"

"My name is Mr Alexander. That is all you need to know about me. I am the head of I.T and school surveillance. You have not been very careful. You have your Genetic Deviation test soon, do you not?"

"I do, Sir," Kat replied, her heart was hammering hard against her ribs. She noted that he was blocking her exit; she knew he would easily overpower her if she tried to fight her way out. She glanced frantically around the room for another escape route.

"I have two options, I could either report you to the authorities, claim a huge reward and never have to work again, or I could help you find a way out of this situation and get you to safety at great personal risk." Mr Alexander said. "Unfortunately, I have already done the former, I'm afraid, and you will have to suffer the consequences." He turned the lock on his side of the door with a click.

He glanced again through the glass pane and looked at his watch. Kat was trying to remain calm;

167

she was desperately trying to think of a way around this; her only exit was the door that Mr Alexander was blocking. She would have to be quick. With her heart hammering, her eyes locked onto the agitated teacher blocking the door, she slowly moved towards the teacher's desk at the front of the room. Keeping him distracted seemed like her only option.

"When did you know?" she asked him, taking a seat at the teacher's desk.

"Quiet. I will not be answering any of your questions." Mr Alexander had his back to the door, armed crossed, watching her with his bright blue eyes. He glanced down at his watch again and tilted his head to look through the door window.

"Who are you waiting for? How many people are coming?" Kat probed again. She started swinging on the chair and used the time to take in her surroundings. The classroom wasn't the biggest. It had three windows and some cupboards at the back of the room, possibly for storing books. There was a stationary holder on the desk, a computer with the school logo as a screensaver gave a bit of light to the room.

Suddenly, a loud buzzing came from the doorway, the teacher took out his phone. Looking up at Kat, he answered it.

"Where are you? I have her here in room 203. Yes, she is alone. 10 minutes? You better be here." He cut off the phone and smiled. Somehow, his once charming face appeared twisted and more ugly in the semi-darkness.

Ten minutes. Kat had ten minutes to get to safety. She had forgotten all about her phone; she slowly pulled it out of her coat pocket and held it in her hands under the desk. She quickly turned the brightness to the lowest setting and typed a text to Jack:

I been caught, was being watched. I have to leave asap. I love you all.

"Give me that phone, now!" Mr Alexander held out his hand. Kat froze; she had a plan. Looking him square in the eyes and pressing send, Kat stood up, showing him the screen. Highlighting the emergency services number and pressing the call button, she looked at him with a smirk on her face.

"You want it? Come and get it." She sounded a lot braver than she felt. The phone rang out for a few seconds before someone answered it at the other end.

"What is your emergency?" the operator asked.

"Help! I am being held, hostage!" Kat shouted as Mr Alexander started towards her. She threw her phone to the back of the classroom towards the cupboards, and he dived after it. Now was her chance; Kat made a dash to the door and pulled at it. She fumbled with the lock and pulled again. He grabbed her round her slim waist from behind and threw her back towards the desk. She hit it hard, knocking the breath out of her. He twisted her around and grabbed her by the throat.

"You will *not* escape. Do you understand?" His hot, coffee breath on her face. "People are paying a hefty sum for you. You will go with them either way, in one piece or many." Kat couldn't breathe, fumbling around on the desk, she felt the scissors in her hand and drove them hard into the neck of the man holding her down.

169

His eyes widened in shock. He let go of Kat's neck, immediately reaching for his own. Horrified at what she had done, Kat stepped back away from him and watched as he pulled out the scissors and fell to his knees. He looked at her, blood seeping through his hands. The man tried to speak, but all Kat could hear was a gurgling sound, nothing more. He fell to the floor in a pool of blood, dead from what Kat could see. She moved closer to him to see if she could hear his breathing, nothing. His phone was buzzing in his pocket, fumbling to get it out. Still vibrating, she tried to unlock it, but her hands shook too much. She reached over to the teacher, rolled him onto his back and felt around for a short while for a pulse, willing him to be alive. Nothing.

She got to her feet unsteadily. Everything felt as if it were a dream. How did she go from eating lunch with her cousin and best friend less than twenty minutes ago to killing a man?

A loud, sudden intake of breath made Kat's heart almost stop. Mr Alexander had taken a breath and had rolled onto his side. He was covered in blood, but the wound where the scissors had pierced his skin had vanished. He had healed and, quickly realising what had happened and where he was, he got to his feet and made another move towards Kat, looking angrier than she had seen anyone.

Kat was frozen to the spot with fear. She did not know how he had survived. He was definitely dead, there was no pulse when she checked, and he definitely was not moving. Maybe he was a Deviant too? He again was between herself and the exit.

She snapped out of her frozen state, turned and ran across the room. She threw her arms over her face and jumped from the window, hitting the concrete path below with a sickening crunch. Her broken bones healed almost instantly, but she still felt the pain for a split second. She lay on the ground for a moment to check everything was in working order, rolled over and saw Mr Alexander look out of the window. He quickly disappeared; she knew he was on the way to get her. She noticed that other students and teachers were peering out of some of the other windows. She could not stay there any longer; she had to run away. She just hoped she would see her family and Ben again someday. The cuts from the glass window had healed instantly, but blood had still sprayed the floor; her clothes were torn and bloody. She ran across the school field, pushing past a couple of students heading toward her, jumped the gate at the bottom of the field and she was gone.

Chapter 25 – Aftermath

As lunchtime drew to a close, Jack and Ben were getting ready to make their way to their afternoon lesson. They saw a couple of students run past them towards the doors to the playground.

"Did you see what happened? She fell from the second floor!" said the taller of the two boys. He pushed open the door, and the two of them continued to run around the building. Jack and Ben watched them through the windows. Jack had received Kat's text and tried to call her back, but the phone had cut off; it went straight to voicemail. The pair exchanged a worried look.

"You don't think...?" Ben started. "That would give her away...." He could feel his chest and heart knot inside, and he was beginning to panic. He could not go back for questioning; he didn't think he would survive this time if he did. More students were sprinting through the cafeteria and heading through the doors. The fire alarm blared suddenly, lights flickered, and the sound of many feet was heading their way. This brought Ben back to his senses, and the two of them stood up.

"We know nothing. We should just follow the crowd. I hope Kat's phone is off. We need to be careful and act normal." Jack said. Ben nodded, and he and Jack headed towards the door. "We need to get to my home as soon as we can, though. We speak to no one if we are questioned."

Ben had turned a pale green colour and was visibly sweating at the mention of questioning. Again, he nodded, and Jack reached for his hand as they headed into the crowd where their classmates were huddled; Ben looked at him, wondering why he had taken hold of him.

"I will not lose my best friend again, Ben," Jack said, looking back and answering his unasked question. "Stay with me and try not to worry," he gave Ben a reassuring smile and pulled him towards some people he knew.

"She jumped out of the window and ran away!" shouted a short, dark-haired girl.

"Who did?" yelled a second, taller girl, chewing gum with braces on her teeth.

"What's going on?" Jack asked one of his classmates, shouting over the noise and confusion. The fire alarm was still ringing very loudly, despite being outside. Sirens could be heard getting closer in the distance. "What's happened?"

"From what I hear, your cousin jumped out of a window in the English corridor. She got up, had blood all over her and ran away. My mate Rob saw her on the floor. No one has seen her since." The boy explained excitedly. "Have you tried phoning her?"

A whistle blew before Jack could answer, everyone fell silent. The teachers had arrived on the playground and organised their students to ensure everyone was accounted for. They all lined up in their classes, and class teachers were taking attendance. Jack's teacher stopped when she called out Kat's name. She looked up and down the row of students and appeared confused.

173

"Jack, where is Kat?" she asked quietly as she stood next to him.

"I don't know where she is, Miss. She isn't answering her phone." Jack replied quietly. She nodded, looking worried. She finished checking off her class names and then headed towards the headteacher, who was standing in the centre of the playground, looking very annoyed. Jack watched the exchange between the two teachers, but neither of them gave anything away in their facial expressions.

Suddenly, a lot of things all happened at once. The fire alarm had been reset, the sirens that headed towards the school turned out to be police cars with darkened windows. Five of them screeched onto the playground, and four officers got out of each one. The headteacher spoke to the officer in charge, who turned to the other officers pointing to the doors. They headed inside the school. A final black car, without sirens, came slowly into the playground, parking next to the police cars. Two men in black suits got out of the car and walked towards the headteacher and the police officer in charge. They were also ushered inside. Everyone on the playground saw this, including Ben, standing behind Jack, who immediately grabbing his hand in fear. The fire alarm sounded again.

"Right, everyone! Thank you for being patient; we have a small issue that needs attending with our fire alarm!" shouted the deputy headteacher through a megaphone. He was tall, had a deep booming voice, and was very friendly, but he looked very agitated and stressed on this occasion. "I ask you all to be patient a little while longer whilst we sort this out. You may sit

174

on the ground in your rows and chat quietly, but I would like you all to stay exactly where you are for the time being."

Jack and Ben exchanged looks and sat on the hard concrete, listening to the chatter between their fellow students. Many of them were confused, some were talking about Kat, some even mentioned her being a Deviant. Some speculated where the blood on the floor had come from; others spoke about the black-suited men. Jack took out his phone again and tried calling Kat. The line was dead.

After about half an hour, a panicked Mr Alexander came running out of the building from one of the fire exits, quickly followed by two police officers. His clothes were covered in blood. One tackled him to the playground floor, whilst the other made a call on his radio then rushed to secure the teacher's arms behind his back. The whole school watched from across the playground. No one made a sound.

"I'm telling you, she stabbed me in the neck!" he shouted, eyes open wide and looking scared. His voice was hoarse from his shouting. "She killed me, I am sure of it! *She* is the one you need to be looking for!" He struggled under the weight of the officer who was holding him down. "Get off me!"

"Isn't that the teacher that took Kat to see the Head?" asked Ben quietly. He got to his feet slowly, so did Jack and many others.

"Yes, it is…" replied Jack. He started walking across the playground; his walk turned into a run. He was angry, beyond furious with him. Whatever he had done to Kat had caused her to reveal herself as a Deviant. She was in a perilous situation, facing it

175

alone now. He was a third of the way across the playground when a figure tackled him from behind, and he crashed to the floor.

"What did you do to her?!" he roared at the teacher, fighting the firm grip of the person now sitting on him. Mr Alexander stopped struggling and looked at him. As did the officers and men in black suits.

"Jack! Stop!" It was Ben. He was sitting on his legs and holding him down. "Do not do this now," he hissed. Everyone is watching. Jack's temper was at its peak. He was beyond reasoning, wanting to hurt this teacher with every fibre of his being.

He could feel an all too familiar pain in his head that he couldn't fight. He knew he was being pulled into a vision.

"Ben…"

He saw armed officers chasing a familiar-looking woman with long brown hair through trees in a flash. She was shot in the back from a distance, with a stun gun and fell to the floor…..then darkness.

Ben had realised very quickly what was going on with Jack, and so he made it out that he was struggling with him, pretended to slip and headbutted him, knocking him out. That way, it would appear to the enthralled audience that they had a bit of a scuffle.

Mr Alexander, meanwhile, continued to shout and protest his innocence as the officers physically carried his struggling, blood-stained frame to one of their cars. They bundled him into the back of the vehicle and slammed the door. The shouting had now turned into a dull murmur.

Ben was just getting up and bringing Jack round when a shadow fell on the two of them. Ben looked up, and with a jolt of fear that caused his heart to chill, he realised it was one of the men in black suits.

"Is everything alright over here?" the man asked. "Does he need any assistance?"

Ben struggled to understand what the man was saying, his heart was thumping loudly in his ears, and a deafening ringing had accompanied it. He looked at the man and blinked, feeling confused.

"Erm, I...I th-think we are okay, thanks," he managed to stutter. The man stared at him for a couple more seconds but looked at Jack when he coughed and opened his eyes.

"Wha-what's going on?" Jack asked. He took a sharp intake of breath and sat up immediately when he saw the man. Their teacher had made their way over to them, and she knelt down next to Jack feeling his forehead.

"Are you alright, Jack?" she asked, concern etched all over her face. Students were now walking across the playground and out of the school gates.

"Yeah, I fell. I think I hit my head." He replied, rubbing the back of his head. "What is that ringing?"

The fire alarm had started up again, Ben helped him to his feet, the man in the black suit walked away. Jack dusted himself off, forgetting all about his anger at Mr Alexander and was now feeling worried for whoever it was in his vision. Their teacher had told them to collect their belongings and head home. School had been dismissed for the rest of the day. It was now officially the weekend. The police cars were just pulling off the playground when they left the site, but the black, darkened car that the men in suits arrived in, was still there.

Chapter 26 – The Search Begins

Jack's mom was waiting for the two boys on her front doorstep when they got home from school. She looked apprehensive and stood up when they got close. She pulled them both into a hug and squeezed them tight.

"I am so glad you are home safe. Are you both alright?" Claire asked, looking carefully at both of their faces.

"We are fine, mom, honest," Jack answered. He did not feel fine, but he also did not feel like going over what he was feeling at this moment. They were all in trouble now, and they needed to come up with a plan in case Kat was found, and in case the authorities decided to look a little deeper into her family and their genetic makeup.

Claire pulled her car keys out of her cardigan pocket and started walking to her car.

"I think we should go and visit your aunt and help her look for Kat," she said, looking at the two of them. "Would you like to come, Ben? Or would you prefer a lift home?"

"I will stay and help you look for her. Kat would do the same for me," Ben replied, feeling determined. He would not let Kat go through what happened to him if he could help it. Especially as she actually *had* a deviance, unlike himself. They were more likely to do worse things to her if they found out that she can heal instantly, he thought. The two boys climbed into the back seat whilst Claire spoke to Ben's mom on the phone.

"Good stuff, let's go then," she said after the call had been made and she had got into the car herself. "Ben, your mom said it was ok for you to stay over night too if you wanted to, of course."

"Thanks, I would like that." He replied.

They pulled up to Kat's house and knocked on the door. Jack's uncle, John, answered. He looked disappointed when he saw that they were at the door and not his daughter.

"Hello, what are you all doing here?" he asked in surprise. He was still wearing his work clothes, his shirt was untucked, and his blue tie was loosened around his neck. Worry was etched into every line in his face. The smile he usually wore when Jack had been to visit previously was nowhere to be seen.

"John, how are you doing? Any news?" Claire asked, "We have come to help you search for Kat. Where is Liz?

He smiled faintly and nodded in thanks. He explained that Liz had gone to the school, asking questions and demanding to know what had happened to her. She had just called him to say that she was going to try and track where she jumped the school gate and that the school would not give her any information about what had happened to their daughter. Claire said their goodbyes and they made their way back to the car

"We will go and meet up with Aunt Liz then?" Jack asked his mom. "More people may be able to spot something that may help."

"Of course, we will, but first, please can you give me your phones?" Claire asked, her hands held out to them both.

"Why? What are you going to do?" asked Jack, handing his phone over.

"We cannot allow people to track us or overhear our conversations." His mother explained.

The three of them were all back into the car and racing back towards the school. As they picked up speed on the main road, Claire threw all their phones out of the window. They spotted Liz just heading into her own car as they finally pulled up to the school. They parked behind her and got out.

"Any luck?" Claire asked her younger sister as she got out of the car. Liz shook her head and started to cry. Claire put her arms around her and held her sister whilst she sobbed. Her whole body quaked as Liz let all her emotions out. She was the sister that usually kept her feelings in check, the one who was able to calm and soothe others around her...

Seeing his aunt so vulnerable and upset made Jack's temper flare up again. He could feel another headache coming on. He looked at Ben, who seemed downcast at what was unfolding around him. Jack could not imagine what he was going through at the moment, but they had to try and find Kat. If having a vision meant that they would be a little closer to finding her, then so be it.

"Ben, keep an eye out for me, please, it's happening again," he said, wearily. He tilted the car seat back as far as it would go and allowed his headache to take over, his mind falling into the vision.

"Okay, be careful," he heard his best friend say, as if from a hundred miles away. Ben closed the car door behind him and sat by his side.

Jack was in a plain room with a large mirror on the wall to his right. He was handcuffed to a metal bar fixed to the table, and a door was in front of him. He felt sore, tired and his wrists were bleeding slightly from the cuffs rubbing. The teacher glanced sideways, and Jack suddenly realised that he was witnessing what was happening to the man that had caused so much chaos this afternoon.

Jack decided that, as he had managed to scream out loud in the vision he had concerning his father, he decided to try and see if he could do the same with this man. He mentally visualised pulling at the cuffs, Mr Alexander did so. Jack tried again, pulling harder, and Jack could feel the teacher's pain, he saw the blood starting to ooze a little faster out of the sores that had been made. He understood in the back of his mind that the pain wasn't his own. The teacher, however, groaned with his effort; his body slumped a little with the release of the pain. The blood quietly dripped into a small puddle on the table, giving Jack a feeling of satisfaction that this man was suffering.

Jack, happy that he seemed able to control things a lot better in this vision, shouted "Let me out!" and was pleased when Mr Alexander did the same. This was how he would get revenge on him for what he did to Kat. He would seal this man's fate. The hatred and anger that surged through Jack were uncontrollable; he would see to it that this man never left this place if he could.

181

A blonde woman in a black dress entered the room, carrying a file. She seemed utterly unaffected by the slowly expanding pool of blood on the table. She sat opposite the teacher and opened the file, looking for a specific page.

"Your name is Mark Alexander, am I correct?" she said in a cool, crisp voice.

"Yes." Mr Alexander answered. He couldn't look the woman in the face, and Jack was aware of the feelings that were coursing through his host's body. Fear, weariness and remorse were the key emotions that flooded his system. Jack felt a little sorry for this man for a moment, he got the feeling that he hadn't meant for things to go so far, but his anger soon returned.

"Give me your account as to what happened at the school this afternoon, Mark," ordered the woman in black, "We will then take a recess whilst we evaluate your testimony and what we are going to do with you."

The woman stared directly at the teacher and listened, without interruption, whilst he gave his version of events, staring at the table. Jack was shocked at what he heard about Kat stabbing him in the neck and even more surprised when he realised that this man had no injuries, save for his wrists. After he finished his account of events, he looked up at the woman and saw her expression unchanged and unreadable.

"Am I free to leave now?" Mr Alexander asked, a little afraid of what would happen if he couldn't go home.

The woman in black put her finger to her ear and looked a little to the left as she appeared to be getting instructions from somewhere. Jack assumed that she must have an earpiece or some form of telecommunication somewhere on her person.

"I think not, Mr Alexander. You appear to be one of the following: you have either lied about being stabbed in the neck, or you have somehow managed to heal your injuries, making it a fair assumption that you are a Deviant." The woman said, standing up and making her way slowly to the door. "So we will be keeping you for further questioning, and we will be running some tests on you to see exactly which one of these you are."

"No. Please. Test the girl. She is the one who is a Deviant; she admitted it herself..." he said weakly.

"Search parties are already in place for the girl, Mr Alexander, so I suggest you worry about your own circumstances. She won't get far." The woman replied. Jack's blood ran cold; they were looking for Kat, he had to say something to try and throw her off the scent.

"Okay, okay, I admit it. I am a deviant. The girl was scared, she did stab me, but I healed. I don't know how, but I did. It was a miracle she fell from the window unharmed. I have been hiding my power for years." Jack quickly blurted out of the teacher's mouth. Jack felt the man's chest tighten in fear and shock as soon as the words fell out of his mouth. The woman froze on the spot in the now open doorway and turned to face him.

"No! I'm lying, that wasn't me!" the teacher shouted. His panic made Jack feel pretty satisfied. He

183

*was now sure that either way, this man's fate was now
sealed. "I DID get stabbed in the neck. It was the
girl!"*

*"Goodbye, Mr Alexander. You have been most
helpful." She said with a nasty smile as she closed the
door. Mr Alexander pulled against his restraints and
roared in frustration, trying to stand up and free
himself. Jack did not know if he had managed to buy
Kat any time, but he did know that Mr Alexander
would not be seeing daylight any time soon. He pulled
back out of the man's thoughts and brought himself
back into his own body and mind.*

"He's awake!" Ben shouted a grin spread across his
face. Jack realised that he had a blanket over him, to
give possible passers-by the illusion that he was just a
sleeping passenger in the back of a car. His head was
pounding, but he ignored it as best as he could. The
car was moving; his aunt had joined them in his
mother's car.

"Where are we going?" he asked, rubbing his
temples. His aunt turned in the front passenger seat to
look at him and held his hand.

*"We have to go somewhere safe, where we can
talk."* His aunt said telepathically. *"I am afraid that
you are not going to be able to go back to school. Tell
us what you saw when we get where we are going. It
will be a couple of hours drive if we manage it."* Jack
nodded in reply and settled into his seat. He saw his
mother keep looking at the rear-view mirror and the
worried expression on her face.

Ben leaned across to Jack and handed him a drink.

"Here, you look like you need it. Your mom
packed supplies. We have clothes and food for a

184

couple of days here." His cheeriness seemed forced. Jack knew that it must be terribly difficult for him. In offering to help his family look for Kat, Ben had now sacrificed seeing his own family again, at least for the time being.

Ben looked out of the window. He was feeling mixed emotions right now; he didn't know how to process all of what had happened. Ben knew he should be feeling upset; leaving his family behind was not easy. However, he could not, and would not, go back under the custody of the law enforcement for "questioning". He had been welcomed with open arms into Jack's family ever since they were both small. They also did what they could to try and set him free when he was taken. He felt that his parents didn't really understand what he went through, but Jack and Kat did. As far as he was concerned, he was with his family now, he cared for these people, and they all cared for him. The fact that he did not have a power was not a problem for them, and they always treated him as an equal.

He looked at the people in the car; Jack had fallen asleep, no doubt his second vision in one day had taken a bit of a toll on him. Liz was staring out of the window. She seemed a million miles away and watched the red sky turn darker over the dusty fields as the sun set behind the rocky terrain. He looked at Claire and noticed that she appeared to be driving pretty fast. She seemed a little distracted and checked her mirrors constantly.

"Claire?" Ben said, leaning forwards slightly.

"Yeah? What's up, Sweetheart?" she replied.

"Any chance we could have some music on, please?" he asked. "It's a little quiet back here."

"Sure, I don't see why not," she answered, flicking on the radio. Music blared loudly, startling Jack awake.

"Sorry!" Ben said. Jack moved around in his seat and mumbled something that Ben couldn't hear. He pulled the blanket up higher around his shoulders, facing away from him this time, and he fell back to sleep.

Ben could just hear the music enough to make out what song was playing, and for a time, it stayed pretty peaceful in the car. Liz had also fallen asleep, and Claire appeared to have settled down into her drive and was making steady progress to wherever it was they were headed.

The sun had finally set. They were now out in the countryside. Red, rocky hills, farmlands and open skies were their companions, with only an occasional car passing by in the opposite direction. Still listening to the radio, Ben heard the music cut off mid-song for a news broadcast.

"Quick! Turn the radio up!" he shouted, waking up both Liz and Jack with a start. Claire turned the dial to hear the newsreader speaking:

We are now conducting round-the-clock searches for the missing student, Kathryn Richards. She is known as "Kat" to friends and family. Kathryn is tall, she has long brown hair and blue eyes. She was last seen wearing a navy school uniform and covered in blood. She is assumed to be a Deviant and therefore very dangerous. We are also looking for some members of her family that also appear to have gone missing. Their Genetic Deviation status is unclear, but their actions lead us to presume that they are also Deviants and thus also extremely dangerous. They are believed to be travelling together, two women and a boy of fourteen, driving a Red '94 Sojourner. If you have any information about the whereabouts of any of these potential Deviants, please call this number....

There was a deadly silence in the car. No one knew what to say for a few moments. It took Liz to break the silence.

"Well, if they are putting a news broadcast out about Kat, it means that she has evaded capture and is not with them." She said optimistically. "That has to count for something, no? And their information isn't all that accurate as they aren't aware that we have Ben here with us too."

"We need to change this car as soon as possible," Claire said, looking at her sister. "We need to stop for gas soon, so maybe we should do it then? Maybe book a motel for the night and try and get one from there?"

"Agreed. This also means that this car is not bugged, right?" Liz pressed on. "Because if it was, they would be tracking us too and know where we are?"

"Maybe, you are right, but we still cannot take that risk. Not until we get a new car." Claire replied. "It's only four miles to the nearest fuel station. I just hope we don't run into any trouble when we get there."

The rest of the car journey was a tense one. Nobody spoke, and no cars passed them by. They pulled up into the gas station, where an attendant was asleep in his booth. There was an empty fast-food restaurant and a motel on the same site. The place seemed deserted; three cars were parked up, one in semi-darkness close to some dense shrubbery.

Claire parked close to one of the cars in the shadows and turned off the engine. She looked at Liz, who nodded some encouragement, and they both opened their doors together. They sneaked over to the car, checked the doors and found it locked. Looking around, Liz found a decent-sized piece of rust coloured rock and hit the back passenger window as hard as she could. The glass shattered and crinkled to the floor. She opened the door, reached the lock on the front passenger door and opened it, climbing inside and unlocking the driver's door for her sister.

The next part was trickier. Neither of the sisters knew how to override the ignition. Claire tried putting her own key into the slot, looking around for inspiration. It was too big. She was suddenly struck with an idea, ran to her car, opened the boot and took out a screwdriver from the toolbox she kept in there.

Running back to the car, she jammed the long, thin screwdriver into the ignition and twisted, it was a long shot, but it was an older model of car, so she had a glimmer of hope it would work. The engine roared to life, the fuel tank was already full, they were ready to go. They both got out of the car. Claire went to get the supplies from her own car and told Jack and Ben to switch vehicles.

"I'll be right back," said Liz, and she rushed off towards one of the other cars, crouching down as she ran.

Claire helped Ben brush the broken glass of the car seat onto the concrete floor. They took a roll of tape out of her repair kit and taped a folded blanket over the broken window. She made sure they had taken everything from her own car and sat in the driver's seat waiting for her sister, who was now doing something to the final vehicle. She came running back with something in her arms, smiling and a little flushed.

"I'll be two more minutes, then we can go," she panted. There was a bit of banging, and a couple of minutes later, she was back in their new car.

"What did you do?" asked Jack.

"I took a license plate from each of the other two cars, but I put one of them on the front of this one, one on the back," Liz explained. "Just in case the authorities decide to try and trace the car we have stolen. It won't last long but may buy us some time if we need it."

Claire started the engine, and they left the station, continuing the journey to the destination that only she and Liz knew about. She knew they were still at least two hours away. She just hoped they would make it.

In all the commotion, the group had not noticed that the attendant had woken up and had watched the group pile out of one car and into the second, covering up the license plates of their new ride. The television in the corner of the office blared with the news of Kat's disappearance. Although the number of people in this group was not the same, he felt three of the four people's descriptions matched. He picked up the office phone...

Chapter 27 – A New Plan

The car journey continued to be uneventful, with very little traffic. Jack and Ben were asleep in the back of the car, a bit more spread out than in Claire's car. This was a far more powerful car with a bigger engine. The radio station stopped the music they were listening to suddenly with another announcement:

We have a new update on our investigation. We are still conducting round-the-clock searches for the missing student, Kathryn Richards. She is known as "Kat" to friends and family. She is tall, she has long brown hair and blue eyes. She was last seen wearing a black school uniform and covered in blood. She is assumed to be a Deviant and therefore very dangerous. We are also looking for some members of her family that also appear to have gone missing. Their Genetic Deviation status is unclear, but their actions lead us to presume that they are also Deviants and thus also extremely dangerous. They are believed to be travelling together, two women and two boys of fourteen, driving a dark blue '91 Rover, heading North. If you have any information about the whereabouts of any of these potential Deviants, please call this number....

The whole atmosphere in the car chilled instantly. They now somehow knew Ben was with them and that they had swapped their vehicle. Liz and Claire glanced at each other. Fear gripped them both; they could lose everything. What if they didn't make it? It was all or nothing. They had no choice but to make it to the safehouse now.

"We need to wake them up and tell them everything, Claire," Liz said quietly. "We can't keep it quiet now. They must know in case anything happens to us, and they have to go alone."

"I know they will make it, though. I have seen it," replied Claire. Liz was gripping the steering wheel pretty tight. Her knuckles were white.

"That's something, I suppose," agreed Liz, "But for my peace of mind, I would like to tell them. Hopefully, Kat will manage to stay hidden and safe. I am so worried about her…" tears had been silently falling down her cheeks. She looked back at the sleeping boys in the back of the car and sighed. Everything about this whole situation was unfair. All of their lives, they had stayed hidden and avoided detection. Liz felt so sorry for her sister. She was in awe of how she appeared to hold everything together despite them being on the run.

Claire had married a man she did not love to make essential connections to keep their children safe. Having to do things she should have never had to do to keep their family safe. This included sacrificing her freedom, for their safety.

"Let them sleep whilst they still can," Claire said, "It is going to be difficult living off the grid. They will need their energy."

The dark roads became darker, surrounded by more wildlife, trees and a pressing silence, broken only by the humming of the car engine. They continued to speed along the roads with Claire eyeing her mirrors, constantly watching for cars.

Jack had woken up with a start; he took in his surroundings and realised they were still driving. It was dark, and no one was speaking. The radio was on a low volume; Ben was still asleep.

"Are we nearly there yet?" he asked his mom and aunt. "It seems like it has been ages...."

"Almost, should be there in about half an hour," Claire answered. "Jack, you need to know a few things...just in case...."

"In case, what?" replied Jack, uncertainty in his voice. "Have you seen something, Mom?" He noticed his aunt sit up a little straighter to look at her sister's face, studying it. She reached over to touch her arm...

"DON'T!" Claire shouted, the car swerving a little as she moved her arm out of the way of her sister's reach. Her shout and the sudden movement of the vehicle had now woken Ben up too.

"You have, haven't you?" Liz said, her eyes narrowing in the darkness. "What is it that you have seen?"

"Never mind, it was nothing, I'm just- I'm driving Liz, you can read my mind later, okay?" Claire tried to sound upbeat and reassuring, hiding her annoyance at being questioned.

A faint rumbling could be heard in the distance; Jack was starting to feel scared. Looking at Ben, he could see the worry on his best friend's face. The rumbling got louder and belonged to a helicopter that could not be seen amongst the thick clouds above.

Suddenly, the car lurched forwards with a crash from behind. A large black car had appeared behind them with no lights on and had smashed into their car, trying to ram it off the road. The car swerved dangerously,and Liz screamed. With a determined look on her face, Claire pushed down harder on the accelerator and continued their way. The vehicle behind struggled to keep up.

"We have to go north, towards the mountains," Claire said, looking at Jack through the rear-view mirror. "If we get split up, you *must* keep heading North. There is a stream. Follow the river's flow until you reach a small bridge and head north about a mile. There is a small cabin, it is very well hidden, but you should see it provided it is daylight, you can rest for a little while there. Head to the mountains from that point."

SMASH! The car behind hit them again. A metallic thud told them that the back bumper had fallen off. An even louder crash told them that the car behind had run over the bumper. Ben looked behind them and saw the car spin and stop.

"It looks like they have burst a tyre!" he shouted, hardly able to believe their luck. "I don't think they are going to follow."

"It is not over yet!" Claire said, glancing again at her mirror. The car had started up again, albeit a little slower than before, and sparks were starting to appear at the base of the front passenger side wheel. "We are going to stop soon. Grab your backpacks and pass mine and Liz's to the front, please. Be ready to run."

Jack reached for the backpacks and handed his aunt their packs.

"How are we going to stop?" he asked. "You said we were only half an hour away from where we needed to be."

"It was half an hour in the car, then we had to take the rest of the journey on foot anyway," Liz explained to her nephew. "He has a point, though. How *are* we going to stop?" she asked, looking at her sister.

A bang, followed by a tinkle of glass, ripped through the car. They ducked in their seats. Claire had her foot pressed down as hard as she could, crashing through the narrow, overgrown dirt road. The men in the car behind were taking shots at their car in an attempt to stop them. The sparks from the missing tyre were lighting up part of the road and making it a little difficult for the man in the passenger seat to aim out of the window.

The helicopter above could now be seen, soaring above them. A spotlight shining from above highlighted the family's position to the aggressive car. Another bang, another bullet whistled through the car, narrowly missing Ben. He felt the bullet whistle past the side of his face, causing his heart to skip a beat. He felt helpless and completely out of control. A third bang and the car span, the engine cut dead, and they all held on tight as the car spun in the darkness into the thick bushes at the side of the road.

"Get out and run!" shouted Liz, "we will be right behind you!" The boys grabbed their bags, swung out of their seats and ran into the darkness together. Liz fumbled for the seatbelt, grabbed her bag and glimpsed at her sister, who did not appear to do the same. It was dark, the helicopter had gone and everywhere was in darkness. A loud, slow whirring seemed to get louder and louder until…

BANG!

Giant fireballs lit up the sky as the helicopter crashed into the woodland about a mile in the opposite direction the boys ran in. In a split second, she could see her sister's face. She could see that Claire had no intention of trying to escape. She had been shot in the left shoulder and was bleeding a lot.

"Claire..." she said, grabbing a cloth from the glove compartment and pressing it down onto her sister's wound. "Hold on, I can get you out...." Fresh tears were stinging her eyes; she couldn't lose her daughter *and* sister on the same day...

"No, Liz. It has to be this way. I have seen it." Claire said groggily. She put her hand on top of her sister's, looked into her eyes and nodded at her. Liz closed her eyes and allowed herself to see and hear what Claire wanted to share with her:

The kids will be alright. Try not to worry. You need to get to the safe point and meet the boys there....I will be alright...I love you.

"I love you too," Liz said out loud, wiping away her tears. The link between them faded as Claire passed out, kissing her sister on the forehead; she got out of the car.

Liz looked around her surroundings. She could see torchlight along the road behind them. Assuming that the men in the black car had survived and were looking for them. She set her backpack firmly onto her shoulders and set off, quickly and quietly in the same direction as Ben and Jack, her heavy heart aching for the two loved ones she may never see again, but her sense of urgency and the fact that the boys still may need her help, urged her onwards.

196

Chapter 28 – The Search For Safety

Jack and Ben ran blindly through the bushes at the edge of the road, scared and disoriented. Moments later, their surroundings were lit up for a couple of seconds from a massive fireball that erupted in the direction they had been running from. They both stopped, gasping for breath.

"We have to keep going. We can't let them catch us," Ben gasped. He was clutching at a stitch in his side but he was determined to carry on to safety.

Jack had crouched down and was looking through his backpack for water already. On the top of the bag, there was a compass and a pair of walking boots, with a note that said *I LOVE YOU*. Jack folded the message carefully and placed it in the inside pocket of his coat.

"She knew what was going to happen." He said, not looking at Ben and turning away from him. He was worried about whether they would find his mother and aunt in the darkness or whether they would even see them again at all. Ben had also crouched down and was rummaging in his own bag, pulling out a brand new pair of walking boots in his own size, in surprise. They both swapped out their school shoes, finding it difficult to believe that they were still in class with Kat that very morning.

"We have to run in this direction," Jack said, pointing North and standing up, brushing off his clothes. "Ready?"

Ben stood up, tightened up the straps on his backpack, looked Jack fiercely in the eyes and nodded.

"Let's go. I'm sure Liz and Claire know where they are going."

The two of them set off at a quick pace. Both boys were pretty fit and, although it was difficult to see too far ahead, their eyes adjusted to the dimness easily. To make sure that they kept heading in the right direction, they ran for periods of what they guessed to be five minutes, and then stopped to check the compass.

After what seemed like an hour, Ben stopped suddenly.

"Wait – can you hear that?" he asked, his head cocked to the side, straining to hear.

"What? I can't hear anything," Jack said, trying to slow down his breathing enough to listen properly.

"Water, I am sure of it. We have to be close to the stream!" Ben said excitedly. "We are going the right way!"

Jack double-checked his compass and nodded in agreement.

"Let's go. We still have a way to go yet," he said, putting his compass back in his pocket. Adjusting his backpack, he started jogging again with Ben by his side.

Unexpectedly, Jack's head seared with a flash of pain. He tripped and fell to the ground. He caught a glimpse of his mother, covered in blood, being taken from their car, her arms being secured behind her back by two men in black suits. One of the men lifted her over his shoulder, carrying her to a second car. He heard a helicopter rumble above them and then Ben calling his name.

"Jack?! Are you alright?" Ben looked at him with concern, hand on his shoulder and shaking him gently. "What do you see?"

Jack's headache had started to fade, and his insides felt like they had been scooped out and dumped somewhere in the forest. They had taken his mother away. Who knew what they were going to do with her now...

"They have taken Mom, just now. I saw it." Jack said, his voice shaking. He couldn't tell whether it was sadness or pure anger causing it. He just hoped that as she was married to his father, they would let her go as soon as possible.

"We must carry on. We need to keep moving," urged Ben. "Or they will have been taken for nothing." Ben was doing his best to try and keep Jack motivated. However, his insides were writhing and squirming with a panic that could not be subdued.

"They?" asked Jack, "It was only my Mom. I did not see Liz at all; she may have escaped."

"That is a small relief then," Ben said, "Try not to worry too much. We will try and get help for Claire." They continued running North in silence, hearing only a faint rumble of a helicopter in the distance.

They eventually reached the stream, following the sound of the water was pretty straightforward as they got closer to it, as the rest of the woods were so still and quiet. It was a fast-flowing stream, moving from the northwest to the southeast, at least ten feet wide and they had no way of knowing how deep it was in the dark. They could not risk wading across. The temperature was already dropping; they did not want to lose the body heat they had generated from running.

The two friends continued to run alongside the water flow, hoping against hope that they had not missed the bridge already. Both of them were starting to feel pretty tired. Neither of them had any way of knowing what time it was as Claire had taken their phones before they had set off.

"Over there!" Jack said, after a time, pointing ahead. They were walking now; they were feeling tired and they could no longer maintain their fast pace. He pointed to a thin, dirty bridge that looked like it used to be painted white many years ago.

They made their way to it and crossed the icy stream. Jack made sure they were facing North again, and they set off once more. Knowing that they were only about a mile from their destination and hopefully some much-needed rest.

The clouds in the sky were heavy; a low rumble could be heard in the distance. Large raindrops started spattering on the coats of the two friends. Pulling up their hoods and quickening their pace once more, they headed North, squinting in the darkness, looking for a small cabin.

The rain got worse, making it harder for Jack and Ben to progress as quickly as they would have liked. It was muddy, and they found it difficult to see much of their surroundings. They sat under an overhanging rock formation for a couple of minutes to drink some water, looking at what other supplies Claire had packed for them.

They carried spare clothes, torches with batteries, a wind-up radio, food and water. Jack also had a first aid kit; Ben was holding a rope.

"I wonder what else she saw...." Ben said, retying his shoelace and looking across at Jack.

"She knew some of what was going to happen this evening at least," Jack replied. He seemed subdued, worried about the consequences of what would happen to his mother. "I wish I could see more. I wish I could control my visions." He punched the ground in frustration.

"Maybe it just comes with time and practise?" offered Ben. "Your mom and aunt seem to be able to control their powers pretty well. You and Kat are just starting to develop yours."

They were silent for a few minutes, listening to the rain, each lost in their own thoughts. They were pulled back to the direness of their situation by the ever-increasing rumble of a helicopter flying above them. From its sound, it was pretty low and not too far away.

"Look!" whispered Jack, shrinking as far under the rock formation as he could. The helicopter had a spotlight and searched the area for them. It was still a distance away, but it wouldn't take them long to be caught up if they didn't find the cabin soon. He just hoped it would be hidden enough from helicopters and other unfriendly eyes until they could decide what their next move would be.

The helicopter started to move further away from their location, and the rain had started to ease a little, so the boys picked up their belongings and headed further North. Jack guessed that they had covered most of the distance required to get to the cabin, so they both started looking around for something that resembled one. They came across a small clearing. Jack was convinced that they were in the correct place, searching it for half an hour, walking around the clearing, but they were unsuccessful.

"Maybe we should move on a little?" Ben suggested. "We may not have gone far enough North."

"Maybe…" agreed Jack. He was just about to set off when he saw what looked like a rusty doorknob in the trunk of an old, twisted tree next to a large rockface. "Hang on a second. What is this?" Jack grabbed the doorknob and turned it. The door swung inside, the smell of damp, musty air invaded their nostrils.

"Let's get inside and lock the door. At least we can dry off a little and wait until daylight here," Ben said, stepping bravely into the dark cabin. It was extremely well hidden and disguised as a tree and rock. Unless you knew what you were looking for, it would be challenging for anyone to find, from the air or the ground, unless you were in precisely the right place.

The cabin was more extensive than it looked on the outside. A small camp bed was along one wall, a tiny gas stove and camping equipment in the far corner and a table with a chair opposite the wall with the bed. Shelves crammed with books were above the bed, and a cupboard was mounted on the wall above the table. There was no window but a tiny air vent in the top corner of the cabin above the door.

Jack and Ben dropped their backpacks and shut the door, closing out the cold and rain. They were able to bolt the door at the top and bottom; a thick piece of wood could be slotted across the door as a barricade, needing all their strength to do so. Feeling slightly safer after blocking the door, they both sat on the bed, in the dark, saying nothing for a while.

Ben, unable to sit still for too long, dug out his torch and decided to check out what was in the cupboard above the table. Cans of food and water bottles were there; they looked like they had been there a while but were still good to eat and drink. Energy bars and chocolate were also on one of the shelves, and they decided to put them in their backpacks, just in case.

Leaving their own food packed in their bags, they ate. They managed to find a large candle in the drawer under the table and some matches. They heated some soup and drank it out of the can using the stove, rounding the meal off with some water and sharing a chocolate bar. The cabin had managed to warm up quite nicely.

"Right, we need to get some sleep if we can," Jack said. "We can share the bed and then have a peek outside in a couple of hours, see where to go from there." He found some blankets under the bed and a sleeping bag mixed in with the camping equipment. Throwing the sleeping bag at Ben and rolling up one of the blankets as a pillow, he settled at the bottom of the bed. "Goodnight," he said and rolled to face the wall.

Ben got into the sleeping bag. He blew out the candle and put his head on the pillow. Staring at the blackness pressing on his eyes. It was the darkest room he had ever slept in. He thought about how long the day had been; so much had happened, and they had all lost so much. He thought of Liz, Claire and

Kat, his heart panged. He cared so much for these kind people, he couldn't understand why they were being hunted for something they couldn't control. He thought of his parents, he didn't even get to say goodbye, he lay there in the dark, unable to sleep, silent tears running down his face…

Jack lay in bed, also wide awake. He was worried about his family and the future that awaited them. Kat was still missing and now so was his aunt. His mother was captured. He and Ben were stuck hiding in a small hut with no plan or anyone that could help. The only information they had was to flee to the mountains. For a second, he thought he heard an animal outside. It seemed to be moving slowly and making low growls. He sat up, listening hard.

"Did you hear that?" Jack whispered.

"Yeah, I did. What was that?" came Ben's reply.

Jack got off the bed, his heart beginning to thump loudly in his ears, and tiptoed towards the door. He fumbled in the dark looking for the matches and lit the candle, setting it on the table. Ben got off the bed too. Carefully, he lifted the chair away from the table, put it in the corner by the door and stood on it. Being the taller of the two, he could see a tiny slither of outside between the gaps in the vent.

"Can you see anything?" Jack asked. Walking towards him, he pressed his head against the door.

"No, nothing, just trees, shadows and rain," Ben whispered back.

"NNYYYGGGHH!" The growling animal was close, very close.

"There! I see something!" Ben whispered. His eyes strained to try and make out what animal it was. Jack moved away from the door and looked for something he could use as a possible weapon if the animal somehow broke in.

"Let. Me. In." A low, familiar voice said at the door. "I'm hurt." Ben's heart lurched.

"Quick!" Ben said, "Help me open the door!" They unlocked the door, and immediately Liz fell forwards onto the pair of them. They caught her just in time. Ben helped her to the bed whilst Jack barricaded and locked the door.

As Ben set her down, he noticed that she was bleeding from a wound on her leg. He bent down to take a look at it. Jack grabbed the first aid kit that was in his pack. The injury was all around Liz's ankle. She looked really pale in the candlelight and was shaking with the cold. Ben threw a blanket over her and lit the stove again, emptying a bottle of water into a pan to heat it. Jack gave his aunt some water and let her recover slightly. He found some painkillers in his first aid kit, he passed a couple to her.

Liz had managed to warm up a little but still looked very pale. Ben brought over the heated water and grabbed another blanket, ripping some strips off it. He dipped one into the hot water and started to clean Liz's wound. It was deep and was still bleeding. He tightly tied a blanket strip around her calf and pressed hard onto Liz's ankle. She screamed in pain, trying to pull her ankle away from him; she didn't have the strength to move it much, falling back onto the bed, he maintained the pressure, Liz passed out.

"How bad is it?" asked Jack, looking anxious.

"Pretty bad, I'd say," Ben replied. He grabbed a fresh strip of the blanket and swapped it for the blood-

206

soaked one he had in his hand. "We have no idea how much blood she has already lost. It looks like she needs stitches."

Liz slept for what could have been at least six hours. Ben had managed to stop the bleeding. Jack stayed awake, sitting in the chair at the table, keeping the first watch over his aunt whilst Ben slept on the floor in the sleeping bag. After what he guessed to be a couple of hours, he woke Ben up and swapped places. Ben had found a box of candles, saving them from using their torches, and the stove was used sparingly. The heat stayed in the room as the only ventilation was the small vent. They had covered the small gap at the bottom of the door to preserve the heat.

When Liz finally awoke, she was groggy and weak. She thanked Jack and Ben for helping her and wrapping up her ankle. Liz explained what happened to Claire and Claire's decision to stay behind. She also told them that she had caught her leg in an animal trap just past the bridge in between laboured breaths. It had taken every bit of her strength to open the trap wide enough to wedge a rock in it to get her ankle out of it. She had stumbled and limped here as quickly as she could in the rain, hoping that the rain would wash away any tracks she had left behind. She went quiet for a little while. The others were patient and let her catch her breath. She closed her eyes and fell asleep once more.

"We will need to make her drink and eat when she wakes up next," Jack said to Ben quietly. He stroked his aunt's face and pulled the blanket a little higher

207

over her shoulder. "We can't stay here forever either; people will be searching for us...."

Ben nodded in agreement and carefully lifted the side of Liz's blanket.

"What are you doing?" Jack asked, "Let her sleep."

"I am checking to see what the time is," Ben whispered. "It is far easier than guessing; Liz wears a watch." It was eleven thirty in the morning. They had both slept for longer than they thought and had completely lost track of time.

"Maybe we should get some sleep too," muttered Jack. "We can't do much else at the moment."

With Liz occupying the bed, the two of them decided to open up the sleeping bag and use that as a base to sleep on, using a blanket to cover themselves. They decided to leave a candle burning, just in case Liz woke up and settled down for a couple of hours rest.

Jack was aware that he was not dreaming. The little details of the room he found himself in were much too clear to be a simple dream. Jack realised that he was in a room that looked like a prison cell. He was lying on his side on a single bunk, staring at the desk opposite him with a metal chair bolted to the floor. He had no window, no furniture and no way of knowing what was going on with the person he shared this vision with.

The door at the end of the room had a small hatch with a ledge on it, presumably for food, and a tiny window above, used for people to check in on the mysterious person. The light was fixed into the ceiling and blindingly bright; no light switch was in the room. He tried to feel how that body was feeling as he lay

208

there. Tired and sore, he realised that this person had suffered some injuries. The pain Jack felt was shooting through his shoulder, and a deep feeling of hopelessness was flooding his senses.

Suddenly, the hatch in the door opened. A pair of cold, black eyes stared through the tiny window.

"Mrs Claire Roberts?" the voice said.

This was his mother! Jack's heart skipped a couple of beats before settling at fast drumming, hard in his throat and ears.

His mother did not move. She did not acknowledge the man addressing her; she needed to rest. She was really hurt.

"Claire Roberts!" the man said again, a little louder this time. Again, Claire did nothing to show the man that she had heard him or was willing to cooperate at all.

A loud click told Jack that the door had been unlocked, and the door swung open. The man with black eyes was also wearing a suit to match. He was tall, broad and foreboding. There was a menacing glint in his eye when he looked down at Claire, who looked him in the eyes with an unwavering stare.

"What do you want?" Claire asked defiantly.

"I have orders to take you with me for questioning."

"Haven't you done enough of that already?" asked Claire. "I have already told you, I will tell you nothing that can be of use to you."

"We shall see about that," the man smirked. He crouched down to her level and stroked the side of her face. "Such a waste...." Claire spat at him in his face and sat up. Pain seared through her shoulder. Jack

could feel anger pulsing through his veins, as well as his mother's.

"Argh!" the man swung his hand in anger and back-handed Claire across the face. Stars sparkled in her vision for a couple of minutes, and the room span. The man grabbed Claire and pulled her to her feet, dragging her out of the room by her hair.

Breathing heavily, Jack opened his eyes. Looking around the room, he saw that both Liz and Ben were awake, sitting on the floor next to him. Liz was holding both his wrist and Ben's hand.

"Did you just see-?" he asked. They both nodded, too stunned to speak. Jack's hands were shaking still with anger, Ben was worried and pale, Liz looked like she was about to faint again.

They were silent for a long time. Ben rummaged through the cupboards and found some canned stew. He heated them a can each for dinner. Sharing bottles of water and another bar of chocolate, Liz broke the silence first.

"Jack, are you going to try again to see what is happening to your mom?" she asked tentatively. "Don't feel like you have to, but if you do, I would like to be there with you, if that is ok?"

Jack had been thinking about what he had seen. He wondered why she was taken and mistreated. She was the wife of an army captain; that had to count for something? Where was his dad? Surely he would have tried to help get her released?

"I will try again, but I can't guarantee I will see anything useful. I can't control who I can see and when." Jack said after a short pause. "Ben, are you going to watch too?"

"I will try. I managed to see what Liz could see earlier. Maybe I can spot something...familiar...that can help." He swallowed. Ben was terrified of what he might see. He did not want to relive his own torture and especially see someone else he cared a great deal for, having to go through the same thing.

"Liz? Are you alright?" Jack moved beside his aunt, concerned. She had slipped a little in her position and was as white as a sheet. She was not in good shape at all.

"I'm okay, Jack, don't worry about me. Just help me back onto the bed. Don't have a vision without me," she said weakly. Her eyes were fluttering, she fell asleep again. Ben lifted the corner of the blanket and saw her ankle had started bleeding again. Her bandage had soaked through.

Jack saw his aunt's ankle, and his heart fell. She appeared to be in worse shape than when she arrived and was still losing a lot of blood. Using her power to see his vision had used up a lot of her energy, and she was struggling. The two of them reapplied fresh bandages, cleaning the wound again and putting pressure on it to stem the flow of blood. Using the small cushion from the chair and a rolled up blanket, they elevated her leg.

"We need help," Ben said, "We cannot stay here another night; Liz needs medical attention that we are unable to give her. We need to try and make a stretcher and make a dash for it before dawn."

"I agree, but we need to know *where* to go. Mom mentioned the mountains. They are miles away, in the North. We could travel at night, but they are huge; how will we know where to head for?" asked Jack

211

sadly. He was worried. Jack couldn't see how things could improve in their current situation. He looked at his aunt again. They were running out of time. "I need to go back into my vision and try and see what is going on. How did you know I was having one?"

"You were mumbling and moaning in your sleep," Ben explained. "Liz touched your wrist and saw what you were seeing; she knew it was a vision. I will keep awake and watch you. If you do the same again, I will wake Liz, then we can see what you see too."

Jack lay down on their makeshift bed again and focused with all his concentration. He had to go back. He had to see what was going on, he had to…

Jack was travelling in the back of a van, wrists tied together, his dad was sitting in front of him. His eyes were downcast, and his usually well-kept hair was untidy and sticking up in places. He had a split lip and a black eye. His father leaned forward and held his mother's hands.

"I am so sorry this has happened, Claire. I could have helped you all. Just tell me what it is that you can do…."

"I can't, Martin. I just can't tell you." Claire mumbled. Her heart completely broken, Jack knew she had given up. There was no way out of this for her that she could see.

"Please, Claire. I may still be able to save you." Jack's dad pressed. "Tell me."

It took Claire a second to realise that he had said "save you," not "save us". She suddenly noticed that his hands weren't tied either. He rubbed his face with a handkerchief, and the cut on his lip disappeared. The black eye faded. The van stopped rocking, and his

212

dad's features changed, suddenly becoming twisted and unfamiliar.

"You will get what you deserve, Claire," Martin growled, grabbing his wife's hair and lifting her off her seat. She winced in pain. "No one makes a fool out of me and gets away with it. I will find the others, with or without your help." He threw her back onto the bench and banged on the van wall. The door opened, and he got out.

Claire's heart was surprisingly calm, despite Jack's battering the inside of his rib cage. Two men opened the doors once more and reached inside for Claire. She stepped out of the van and was pushed into a large white building.

Once inside, she could hear the chatter of many voices, laughing and joking. She was escorted down a narrow corridor and down a flight of stairs. She saw a sign labelled DRESSING ROOM and was told to wait inside. She was pushed through the door. It was closed behind her. Jack saw dressing tables with lights all around wooden boards, where mirrors used to be. An elderly woman came up to her with a tape measure around her neck. She took a quick measurement of the length of her body from her shoulders to her knees and disappeared.

Returning after a minute or so, she gave her an outfit and told her to change. Claire obliged. The material was coarse, a horrible shade of green. It made her soft skin itch.

"Right, it's off to make-up for you now, dear, I'm afraid," the old lady said, not meeting her eyes. "Just through this door and into the next room, please."

213

Claire and Jack wandered, confused, into the next room where there were chairs in a row with an attendant at each chair. Each one of them refused to meet her questioning gaze, and she could see no make-up insight.

"Take a seat here, please," a young man closest to the next door said, gesturing for her to take a seat in his chair. "We will be less than five minutes."

Claire slowly walked across the room. Everyone's eyes were on her. Where was everyone else? She wondered to herself. Again, she sat in the chair in front of a dressing table with no mirrors. The man attending her told her to open wide, she did. Suddenly, she felt a sharp pain in the corners of her mouth as they were stretched into an uncomfortable position from behind. She raised her hands to pull off what he had applied to her face, and two other attendants held her arms out to her sides, whilst a rod was threaded into her clothes from behind, making her shoulder scream out in pain.

Jack had a horrible feeling he knew where this was going. However, he owed it to his mother and himself to see this vision out to its end. His mother was told to stand up, she refused. She was then dragged to her feet and out into the next room.

This room was pitch black. He felt people attach things to his mother's arms and ankles. The pole running through her clothes was also connected to the back of her head. Jack's heart had almost crashed through his chest. He hoped with all his heart that he was wrong. He hoped that the others had not managed to see that he had a vision. He hoped that something would happen to save his mother by some miracle.

214

Light, cheery and horribly familiar music began as lights were switched on. Looking as far to the left and right as she could, she could see that others were attached to her poles. With a horrifying jolt, she saw that their mouths were also pinned back into a twisted smile.

Their platform rose slowly up onto a stage, in front of a live audience. Jack could feel his mother thinking about him, about how much she loved him and that she hoped he would be ok. She looked into the crowd and saw some soldiers that worked with her husband laughing and jeering. Her body was being pulled into doing some sort of dance. The more she fought it, the harder and more painful it became. Scanning the crowd, just as the music was starting to draw to its conclusion, she saw him, laughing and drinking, looking at her. Her husband! Claire, and the others on the stage, all bent forwards to take a bow. Darkness engulfed Jack, suffocating and pressing on him from all sides. Claire Roberts, his mother, was dead.

Jack woke up, tears streaming down his face. He had just watched his mother be murdered whilst his father had sat and watched. Clearly, his reputation and image meant more to him than his own family. A fury was coursing around Jack's body as nothing had ever done before. He was shaking. He looked to his best friend, who also had tear tracks on his cheeks, but he wasn't looking at Jack. He was holding Liz's hand with his head bowed.

Looking at his aunt, who had clearly been holding his hand whilst he had his vision, he could see that she too was no longer with them. Her skin had turned an ashen grey, and she was not breathing.

215

"Oh, Liz," Jack said, sobbing. "I am so sorry." He knelt forward, holding her hand, and wept.

"She died just as your mother did," Ben explained and he put his arm around his best friend. The pair of them sat by Liz's side, mourning the death of both sisters. They both stayed in this position for over an hour before either of them moved.

"I don't think I can take much more of this, Ben," Jack said, wiping his eyes. "First Kat, then Mom, now Liz...How many more people have to die before we can be safe? We need to go. We can't stay here now."

The pair of them gathered their things, cramming as much food and water into their backpacks as they could carry. They changed out of their school clothes, noting they hadn't changed their clothes in a couple of days, leaving them behind in a neat pile.

"Hang on a second, we haven't looked at Liz's pack," Ben said. "She may be carrying something useful." Ben took out clothes and a compass from Liz's belongings. A picture taken at Kat's seventh birthday party of the whole family was carefully folded inside one of the inside pockets. Ben handed it to Jack, who put it in his pocket with the note from his mother. There was also a map, some bandages and a torch with some spare batteries, which they also took.

They arranged for Liz to look as if she were sleeping, she seemed to have a calm look on her face, and they tucked a blanket around her. Leaving a fresh candle lit on the desk as a vigil next to her, Jack bent down to kiss his aunt on the forehead.

"Goodbye, Aunty Liz. I love you." He whispered. Ben stroked Liz's hand, removing her watch and kissed her on the forehead too, also saying goodbye.

216

Having to leave her behind after expecting her to be with them, to help guide them, crushed their already devastated spirits. With heavy hearts, they both took one last look at her in the doorway, and they left.

Looking at Liz's watch, the time was now just after four o'clock. The sun wouldn't set for at least another couple of hours. They moved North under the cover of trees for as long as they could, stopping every now and again because Ben was convinced he could hear something in the distance. Not seeing above the trees made things a little better as he hoped they would not be seen from the air either.

Jack was struggling to come to terms with the losses he had just witnessed. His body seemed to be on auto-pilot. His mind was completely numb. He could hear Ben talking to him but could not come up with any form of response. He couldn't speak; he just wanted to go home. He wanted things to be how they were just forty-eight hours ago. Before Kat jumped out of that window and when they weren't being hunted…

"Listen!" Ben said, frustration in his voice. Jack realised he must have been talking to him for a short while before he snapped out of his thoughts for a moment.

"What?" he asked. "Sorry, I…"

"SHHH!" Ben said, pulling Jack into a crouch and hiding behind a large tree trunk. "I have been hearing faint noises coming from far behind us every now and again. A rumbling sound, maybe vehicles. I think they are getting closer to finding us."

They continued to walk along the undergrowth. The trees were starting to thin out a bit now. However, darkness was creeping in as the sun set, making it harder to see their route. A rumble could be heard in the distance. The two boys looked at each other, feeling scared and alone. Helicopters were searching far behind them, with spotlights lighting up the dark. Thankfully they were still in the distance, but nonetheless, they still had to be vigilant.

Jack decided to examine the map they had taken from Liz's pack. He spread it out on the floor, sheltering behind some large rocks and used his torch to take a quick look. Ben crouched down next to him, looking too, covering their heads with their jackets to stop the spread of the light. Trying to first find the bridge they crossed the day before, they followed the map North and found a small clearing in the trees that could have been where the cabin was located. On closer inspection, they noticed a small red dot on the map in that clearing that looked like it had been marked with a pen. It was hardly noticeable. They followed the map to where they thought they were and found nothing except woodland. They noticed that the land got steeper a little further ahead, but the mountains were miles away. At least a couple of weeks walking, they guessed, they could not even be seen from where they were at that moment.

The rumbling of the helicopters as they circled again seemed to be drawing ever closer to their location. Jack grabbed the corner of the map and started folding it away when Ben grabbed his wrist.

"Wait, look!" he said, pointing to the map.

"Where?" asked Jack, squinting down at the paper.

"Here," Ben said excitedly, pointing at a road that was not too far away from where they guessed their rough location was. "I think we should head for the road."

"Why?" Jack questioned, "We are more likely to be discovered on the road." He was feeling irritable and wanted time to be alone to grieve. The last thing he wanted to be doing right now was traipsing through the wilderness to somewhere, just because Ben thought it was a good idea.

"Look more carefully," Ben said to his best friend. "Right *here.*" He pointed at the map. Jack leaned in close to the map and saw what Ben was referring to. Another red dot. This made him more certain that his mother had seen a lot more to their escape than she let on. That she knew what was in store for them and that she knew her fate before she even got into the car. Yet she still did it to keep him and Ben safe.

"Right, we head for the road," Jack agreed, turning off his torch and standing up, stuffing the map into his pocket. Overhead, another helicopter hovered, shining a spotlight through the trees. They heard men shouting in the distance and dogs barking. It was too close for comfort now. They had no choice but to run for it.

They checked which direction they thought the road was in and ran. Pure adrenaline kept the two friends running for the road for at least half an hour. The voices and the helicopter had faded a little into the distance but could still be heard. They were starting to get pretty tired now; the darkness had truly set in.

"I have to have a quick break," Jack said. "I am so tired." His visions had taken an enormous toll on him, and with all the running they were doing, it was apparent he needed a short rest. Jack receded into his

220

own mind, thinking about all of the happy times he shared with his mom and his aunt. He could feel the sharp sting of tears in his eyes, all the happy times he shared with his cousin... He had lost three people he deeply cared for, three people that could do extraordinary things that could have helped so many others. Three people who had to hide part of their true selves because the government was afraid of them. He vowed to get vengeance on them and make them pay. The retribution would begin with his father.

Suddenly, the place where they had stopped to rest was lit up brighter than a star for a second, maybe two. Their eyes met with a shared terror, frozen to the spot. The searchlight moved again. Jack and Ben grabbed their belongings once more and sprinted towards the road, the helicopter hovering above them, still searching. The light sometimes crossed the path ahead of them or to their side as they ran. They were confident that they hadn't been seen through the trees.

A second and third helicopter seemed to join the first, swooping around in the area they were travelling through. The pursuers must have worked out how fast they could have travelled and made it their priority place to search. The noise was deafening, the lights were frequently crossing their path now, and Jack and Ben were starting to get desperate.

Shouting and lights on the ground were also within their sights now. Men were walking through the trees, calling their names and shining torches. With their hearts hammering, they were stumbling a little as they fled. Their route started to incline as the map said it would, meaning they were getting very close to the road. The helicopters were circling the area, looking

221

for the slightest movement or glimpse of either of the two boys. The noise was deafening.

Jack and Ben had stopped for a few seconds to catch their breath, both of them clutching at stitches in their sides and needing to take a drink of water. Jack was just putting Ben's bottle back in his backpack when they were both lit up by torchlight.

"Over here!" A deep voice shouted into the surrounding darkness, "I can see them up ahead!"

Sheer panic entered their systems, the surrounding area went into darkness. The helicopter propellors were slowing down. Men were making indistinguishable, confused shouts to each other; some of them sounded scared. Jack and Ben continued running. They could not get captured now, not after what was sacrificed to get them this far.

Unexpectedly, they reached the road. A set of headlights was heading towards them at a breakneck speed. The lights belonged to a dark green van that screeched to a standstill a few metres past them. The boys stopped running and, gasping and clutching at their sides, they stared at the truck. Three massive explosions happened behind them as the helicopters fell out of the sky, the fireballs lit up the entire road.

The back doors of the van opened, Kat was standing there, holding them open with a grin on her face. The grin rapidly disappeared when she saw their faces.

"Get over here! Get in the van!" she shouted.

The two boys could not believe their eyes; they ran to the van and jumped in, Kat closing the doors behind them. Banging on the side of the vehicle, it sped off. She turned to look at them both, her sharp eyes noticing immediately that something was wrong, "What the hell has happened?" she asked.

THE END

Printed in Poland
by Amazon Fulfillment
Poland Sp. z o.o., Wrocław
17 August 2022

6182ab3d-1fc8-4d35-ab2a-e3ce17faf56aR01